Swansong

VANDANA KUMARI JENA

RUPA

Published by
Rupa Publications India Pvt. Ltd 2025
161-B/4, Gulmohar House,
Yusuf Sarai Community Centre,
New Delhi 110049

Sales centres:
Bengaluru Chennai
Hyderabad Kolkata Mumbai

This is a work of fiction. Names, characters, places and incidents are either the product of the author's imagination or are used fictitiously and any resemblance to any actual person, living or dead, events or locales is entirely coincidental.

P-ISBN: 978-93-7003-286-6
E-ISBN: 978-93-7003-049-7

First impression 2025

10 9 8 7 6 5 4 3 2 1

Printed in India

Swansong

Vandana Kumari Jena is a retired officer of the Indian Administrative Service. She writes novels, short stories and poems. Her short stories have been published in over twenty anthologies.

Her works include two novels—*The Dance of Death* (2008) and *Clueless* (2019); four collections of short stories—*The Incubation Chamber* (2014), *The Future is Mine* (2015), *One Rotten Apple and Other Stories* (2018) and *Over the Edge* (2022); and a collection of middles—*In the Middle* (2015).

Vandana lives in Mumbai.

Also by Vandana Kumari Jena

Over the Edge

To the special boys in my life—
my sons, Prakrit and Ankit,
and my grandson, Alexander.

You are the light that illuminates my world,
the brightness and warmth that keep me strong and
moving forward with purpose.

Keep shining...

Contents

1. Swansong	1
2. The Dark Night	19
3. The Parcel	25
4. Maya	31
5. Father and Son	40
6. The Amish Quilt	47
7. Redemption	53
8. Second Honeymoon	61
9. Climb Every Mountain	71
10. Revathi	79
11. Trust, Borrowed and Broken	84
12. Childhood Monsters	91
13. The Boy Next Door	98
14. The Sound of Silence	107
15. The Wait	116
16. Coming Home	124

17. Dying Embers 130
18. Cardiac Arrest 136
19. Memories of Happier Times 142
20. Up in Smoke 151
21. Roosevelt Island 159
22. Angel of Mercy 167
23. The Murder I Solved 174
24. Why Did I Forget? 187

1

Swansong

I never knew my mother could move so swiftly. Not like that. Not like an eagle swooping upon prey. Or like a dove escaping the claws of a swooping eagle. She was as graceful as a swan as she glided over the ground—as though it were a pool of glistening water and not a slab of concrete. She reminded me of Anna Pavlova in the famous ballet *The Dying Swan*, excerpts of which I had only seen on television.

She surprised me. I had always thought she was like a rabbit, a scared rabbit that looked over her shoulder ever so often when walking on the road, eyes darting surreptitiously, as though she were afraid of a mysterious stalker. But that day she almost glided up the concrete and leapt into the air, like a dove in flight. We all stood frozen, shocked into silence, watching her plunge into the valley. She must have held on to the ledge and jumped, but it did not seem so. Rather, as I said, she simply glided across the floor and leapt into the air. We ran to the edge and looked down. I could not have heard the sickening crunch of her head hitting the rocks below, yet I could almost swear I did. I could not have seen her blood splashed on the rocks, but I felt certain that I had. My mind flew back to that morning when Ma had beamed with delight as she wished me happy birthday. It was a special one. I had just turned eighteen. She asked how I wished to celebrate, and I said impulsively, 'Let us go to Tiger Point and then have lunch.'

Her face clouded for a minute. She did not like public places. But then it cleared. She said, 'It's your birthday, Princess, we shall do what you want.'

It was a term of endearment she had used when I was a child. Not any more. But she used it today. I knew she was happy, not only because it was my birthday, but also because I had secured admission to an engineering college in Lonavala itself. My classes were going to start soon. Standing there with her, I had felt blessed. But now the nightmare had begun.

I found my voice and began to scream. It was an anguished cry, like that of a *rudali*—a professional mourner, paid to cry when someone dies. My screams rose to a crescendo and must have alerted the police van I had seen parked outside Tiger Point. I soon saw a couple of men in khaki running towards me. They probably suspected that I was being assaulted. I pointed at the man who had called out to my mother and said, 'Arrest him. He killed my mother.'

'He killed my mother! He killed my mother!' I kept repeating, my voice hysterical and strident by turns. 'He killed her!'

The groups of tourists who had come for sightseeing looked shocked. The man I was accusing had been nowhere near her. There was no way he could have killed her. Everyone had heard him say 'Chhavi?'—a little tentatively—when he saw her.

And she, instead of replying 'I am not Chhavi, I am Palash,' had whispered 'Suyash?' and then stood still. As he walked towards her, she glided across the path and leapt into the air.

We were all witnesses to what had happened. A murmur of dissent followed my plea to the police. Suddenly there was a babble of voices as the crowd tried to attract the policemen's attention. However, Suyash remained silent. One of the policemen asked him to accompany them to the police station. Suyash looked bemused. The expression on his face seemed to irritate the officers. I too accompanied them, benumbed after the incident, the realization that my mother had leapt to her death not yet sunk in.

The police station was not far from Tiger Point. The policemen bundled Suyash into a jeep while I sat at the back. I turned and saw some of the visitors walking behind us.

'Voyeurs,' I muttered in disgust. I entered the police station with trepidation. I had never been inside one before. I wondered how many eighteen-year-old girls had. There was something very intimidating about it. Maybe it was the way the police officer on duty looked. He appeared grim and saturnine, glaring suspiciously at both Suyash and me. Perhaps, in his job, he had learnt to suspect everyone. He offered no word of commiseration. For him, my mother was another case—unsolved as yet. If it had been suicide, he could have closed the file quickly. But I had alleged murder. That complicated things.

'I want to lodge an FIR against him,' I said to the officer. 'He killed my mother.'

The fact of her death had not really registered. I was in shock, though I did not realize it.

'The eyewitnesses said he was nowhere near her,' protested

the policeman who had accompanied Suyash.

Suyash remained silent, saying nothing in his own defence, as though he were merely a bystander watching a street brawl.

'What is the basis of your accusation?' the police officer asked me, his eyes dark with suspicion.

Before I could answer, a tourist—one who had been clicking photographs at Tiger Point with his iPhone—arrived at the station. 'I was making a video, and I have accidentally caught the entire incident on camera,' he said.

The Station House Officer squinted and watched the video intently. 'Well, it seems clear that this gentleman was nowhere near your mother and did not push her. She jumped of her own accord,' he pronounced.

'But he called her Chhavi, and she took fright and jumped,' I said. 'He provoked her into committing suicide, in which case, you should book him for abetment to suicide.'

The officer raised his head, a little startled that I knew about abetment to suicide. He then turned towards Suyash. 'Well?' he asked, a trifle impatiently.

'I thought she was Chhavi, a woman I knew in Delhi,' Suyash replied. 'I had no idea she would react this way.'

The officer continued to look at him unblinkingly, perhaps hoping to unnerve him.

Suyash stared back. The officer was disconcerted. Perhaps he was used to people lowering their eyes, looking abashed. Suyash then took out a business card from his wallet and handed it over. The officer looked at it for a minute. Suddenly he underwent a transformation.

'Sir,' he said deferentially, getting up and saluting.

Obviously a political bigwig, I thought contemptuously. *Even the police are not exempt from their influence.*

'Sorry for the inconvenience, Sir,' said the officer. 'You are free to go.'

I watched open-mouthed as Suyash turned to leave. At the door, he paused and said, 'This girl, whatever her name is, has no *locus standi* to lodge a complaint.'

'What?' The officer looked shocked, as did I.

'She is not her daughter,' said Suyash, his voice cold. 'The woman who died was not her mother.'

'What do you mean by that?' I spluttered.

'Take a DNA test if you want. It will prove that I am right,' he said as a parting shot.

'Well, miss, what proof do you have that she was your mother?' the officer asked, seemingly taking his cue from Suyash's allegation, absurd though it was.

I opened my purse and took out my Aadhaar card—the proof of identity I usually carried.

The officer sneered. 'This does not have your mother's name on it. Don't you have a passport?'

'I don't have a passport, and even if I did, I wouldn't carry it around casually, would I?' I said sarcastically.

We had reached a stalemate. I thanked God that Ma had left her handbag behind when she leapt to her death—otherwise my troubles would have been compounded. Her handbag had her Aadhaar card, with her name, Palash Sanyal, on it. But of course, it would not establish that I was her daughter. I broke out in a sweat, wondering how I could prove that the woman who had jumped was my mother.

Then I suddenly remembered—'My mother's name is on my CBSE marksheet,' I said. 'I passed Class XII this year.'

'Give me your roll number,' he said.

Thankfully, I had a good memory and remembered it. He

instructed his computer operator to open the CBSE website. We waited tensely as he scrolled down my name.

'Mala Sanyal. Mother's name: Palash Sanyal,' said the officer, sounding disappointed.

Suddenly, the enormity of what had just happened struck me and the reaction set in. My mother had killed herself.

Her body had been sent for post-mortem. I had not seen it yet. I did not want to—certainly not when it was broken and bloodied. I knew that not even a miracle could have saved her. I had seen her blood-stained face with my own eyes.

I was all alone in this world. An orphan. I had just turned eighteen and had no relatives, and very few friends. How would I survive?

The police officer saw me looking faint and told me to sit down. 'You're in shock,' he said. 'Have a cup of tea.'

He hollered to a boy carrying cups of tea on a tray, and soon a steaming cup was placed before me. 'Drink it,' he said gruffly, his voice unexpectedly kind. 'It will make you feel better.'

'Nothing can,' I said under my breath.

Suddenly I began to bawl. A lady constable came and began crooning to me as I sobbed my heart out. Perhaps she realized I was devastated.

The officer sent me home in a police jeep. I think he was afraid that, left to myself, I too would jump. After all, madness tends to run in families.

I sat in the front seat beside the driver, while the policewoman sat in the back. I looked straight ahead, but all I could remember was our journey to Tiger Point that morning.

It had been a long ride. The taxi must have been expensive, but Ma had not wanted to spare any expense for my birthday.

After all, I had not asked her for the moon—just a visit to Tiger Point.

There was nothing particularly exciting about it. It was only a viewpoint, but on the rare occasions I had gone there with her, the scene below had always left me breathless. I loved sitting on the wooden bench near the shacks that sold *kanda bhaji*—crisp onion pakoras—along with tumblers of hot masala chai. There was something very liberating about seeing the vast expanse all around.

That morning, as we stood at the edge of Tiger Point and looked down, a tentative smile had played on Ma's lips, as though she were afraid to throw her head back and laugh loudly. When had Ma ever laughed with gay abandon? I did not know.

We had just left the ledge and were returning when the man who called himself Suyash called out to her.

Why did Ma jump? What sort of hold did Suyash have over her? And how had she leapt so high? *She must have held a state record in high jump*, I mused. Why had the authorities not barricaded the area? If they had, Ma would still be alive.

We were still far from home. I spent the rest of the journey looking out at various points from where I, too, could take a leap. At eighteen, I had no idea how I would live my life alone.

The policewoman dropped me home but instead of going away, she hovered at the doorstep while I fumbled in my purse for the key. She then looked at me and asked, 'Is there no one at home?'

I shook my head.

She sighed. 'Let me make you a cup of tea.'

I realized she did not trust me enough to leave me alone. Fortunately for her, just after she gave me a cup of tea, we heard a persistent knock at the door. From the peephole I saw my neighbour, Dixit Aunty, standing outside with a plate of pakoras.

I opened the door reluctantly. I did not know her well. I remembered there had been some scandal concerning her. Ma had always tried to avoid her. She hastily set the plate on a side table and held me tight, almost smothering me.

'How did you come to know?' I asked faintly.

'It is all over the local news,' she said candidly, and I wondered if she took ghoulish delight in the way Ma had died. But I was doing her an injustice. I knew she was trying, in her own way, to be kind.

The policewoman was relieved to see her. She hastily grabbed a pakora Dixit Aunty offered and left.

Dixit Aunty insisted I spend the night with her. Perhaps, like the officer, she too was afraid that—like my mother—I might jump. I did not resist.

Just as I was about to leave, there was another knock. Dixit Aunty opened the door and I saw Ma's colleagues from the library standing at the doorstep.

News travels fast—and bad news travels faster. Were they all vultures? I knew I was being paranoid. I looked at Ravi Uncle. His eyes were red-rimmed. It confirmed my suspicion that he had been fond of Ma. Perhaps they had been lovers. Who knew?

He sat on a straight-backed chair, his head bowed, saying nothing. Ma's other colleagues, however, offered words of commiseration.

'Don't worry, Mala,' said Ravi Uncle after some time. 'We will make all the arrangements.'

'Arrangements?' I realized with horror that he was talking about her cremation. It brought a fresh bout of tears to my eyes.

'I don't think you will be able to manage it. I think we should cremate Palash in an electric crematorium,' he said.

He waited for me to say something. I did not know what to say. I really had no idea what Ma would have wanted. We had never spoken about it. She had not expected to die so soon. In the end I just nodded.

'There is none in Lonavala. We will have to go to Pune. I will book the crematorium and arrange for transportation,' he said in a rush. I realized he must have rehearsed those words. He seemed as affected by Ma's death as I was.

After they left, Dixit Aunty held me firmly by the hand and took me to her house. 'From now on, you will stay at night with me. I will take care of all your meals. In any case you are not supposed to cook until…' Her voice trailed off.

I looked at her in surprise. I did not know her well, though our families were among the oldest residents in the colony. Ma had never been particularly warm towards her. How little we know of our neighbours. Or friends!

I sat in Dixit Aunty's house, my mind in a whirl. I began to cry again, and the tears just wouldn't stop. Suddenly I remembered Suyash's insinuation.

'This girl has no locus standi. The woman who died was not her mother.' The words pounded in my head. What did he mean by that? He had suggested a DNA test. But why?

I decided mutinously that I wouldn't take it. It would feel like betraying my mother.

'What is the matter?' asked Dixit Aunty. 'What is troubling you?'

I bit my lip. I was not willing to share that sordid exchange with her—after all, she was still a stranger.

'Whatever it is, you will have to face it, and face it alone, Mala,' she said.

She was right, of course. I narrated the entire incident to

her, leaving out nothing, not even his parting shot, which had shaken me to the core. She listened calmly, her face entirely expressionless.

'There are always secrets in a person's life. And scandals as well. But one learns to live with them…' she said. After a while she added, 'You may have been too young, but you must have heard of a scandal concerning me.'

I bowed my head. I had heard something.

'I had an affair. I was trapped in an abusive marriage. My husband used me as a punching bag… It is easy to stray in a loveless marriage,' she said ruminatively. 'I found someone else. I decided to spend my life with him. He was my son's tutor. But my husband found out. And beat him to death.'

She fell silent. After a while she said, 'I think I know who told him.'

I realized she was referring to her son.

'My husband is now in jail. But everyone blames me. They all sympathize with him. Murder can be forgiven, but not adultery,' she said fatalistically. 'I dread the day he gets out.'

'It has been difficult for me to live here. But where can I go? I have learnt to take each day as it comes. I am sure your mother's story will not be as bad as mine,' she said.

∽

Ma's body was released the next day. Just as we were about to leave for the cremation, I found my friend Sneha at the door. Behind her stood my other classmates from school. Each one hugged me and cried. I realized that I could have had many friends, if only my mother had allowed me to make them.

Once the cremation was over, I wondered how I would live without Ma. Nothing would fill the vacuum her death had caused. Then I began to think about how I would survive. I knew nothing about the state of Ma's finances. I would need to go to the bank to find out.

Ravi Uncle came and told me that my mother had left behind a will, and I was the sole beneficiary under it. She had left me the house, her money and her jewellery that was in the bank locker. My entire education could easily be financed with what she had left behind.

I wondered why Ma had felt the need to make a will. After all, I was her only child. Everything would have come to me anyway. Why the need for a will?

I asked Ravi Uncle.

He began to fidget. 'I asked your mother the same thing, but she was adamant,' he said.

Once again, I remembered Suyash's allegation. He had suggested a DNA test. I decided to get it done.

Lonavala was a small town, with no such facilities. I wondered how I would go about it. I decided to ask Ravi Uncle. If he wondered why I wanted to find out about DNA testing, he did not show it. He gave me the details of a hospital in Pune and even offered to accompany me. I was grateful for his offer. I wondered once again if he had had feelings for Ma.

∽

I carried Ma's hair for the DNA test—there was plenty in her hairbrush. She had been complaining of hair fall for months.

The wait for the results was tense. When the report arrived at last, I opened it eagerly—and felt devastated as I read it.

Suyash had been right. I was not my mother's daughter.

As I sat with the report in my hand, I wondered if I had ever truly known my mother. Who was she—Chhavi, as Suyash had called her, or Palash, as she had told me?

I remembered her words: 'Your father's name was Parijat. It means a flower in heaven; and my name is Palash—the flame of the forest. We were a match made in heaven.'

Now I knew her name could not have been Palash—otherwise she would not have jumped when Suyash called her 'Chhavi'.

What was the mystery behind it? Did I know her at all—the woman who had claimed to be my mother, but was not?

I wondered what had gone on in her life that I knew nothing about. I had believed she led a humdrum existence—worked in a public library, buried herself in books. I had no idea she was keeping a secret of such magnitude.

Who was I? Who was she? What was the truth about us? I needed answers.

I needed to meet Suyash. But I had no idea where he lived. I realized I had no choice but to visit the police station again.

'I can't give you his address,' said the SHO truculently. 'You will start harassing him.'

I looked at him in desperation. 'He is the key to this mystery. He knows the truth about me. He knew my mother as Chhavi. He also said she was not my mother. Only he can tell me who I really am.'

Perhaps the officer saw the desperation in my eyes. He relented, handing me Suyash's business card. He was the Commissioner of Income Tax.

No wonder the SHO had saluted him, I thought sourly.

He then scribbled the address for me. I looked at the piece of paper and groaned. Suyash lived in Pune. I had already gone there for Ma's cremation and then again for the DNA test. Now I would have to go there once again, and this time, alone.

The next morning, I caught a bus to Pune.

I took an autorickshaw to Suyash's house. He lived in a palatial bungalow. I looked at the sprawling lawns as I walked up to the portico and rang the bell.

Suyash opened the door himself. His face was grim, his eyes bleak. 'You?' he said, his voice incredulous. 'How did you get here?'

My heart sank. I was clearly unwelcome. Obviously, the fact that I had accused him of murder still rankled.

'You were right,' I blurted. 'I took a DNA test. The report shows that I am not my mother's daughter.'

He did not respond.

'Who am I?' I asked desperately. 'And who was she?'

He shrugged. 'Find out, if you want,' he said indifferently. 'I know Chhavi kept a diary—at least she used to. Habits like that do not die. I am sure she poured her heart out into it.'

I turned away, dejected by his refusal to help. Why was he so reluctant to tell me the truth? How did he know my mother? Had they been friends? Or lovers?

If I was not her daughter, whose daughter was I? Throughout the return journey, I brooded. Once home, I realized I was starving. Suyash had not even offered a glass of water. I was too tired to even make Maggi noodles.

Once again Dixit Aunty proved to be my saviour. She brought me a plate of chicken biryani and I fell on it hungrily. Afterwards, I crawled into bed and slept. I had not known the truth about myself for eighteen long years. I could wait another day to discover it.

The next morning, I decided to begin my search for Ma's diaries. She had been a hoarder. The thought of going through all her trunks and suitcases appalled me. But I had to.

After four hours of fruitless search, I remembered that Ma's bed was a box divan. I quickly removed the mattress and opened it. It was full of diaries. I browsed slowly, stopping when I saw my name.

'Mala is not my daughter,' she had written. 'She is the child I stole.'

I was astounded. Steal a child? How could one do that?

Was she a nurse or nanny who had taken me as an infant? Or a childless woman unable to bear children?

Tears rolled down my cheeks—hot, molten tears that could not purge my grief.

'How could I steal someone else's child and disappear?' she had written on another page. 'How could I leave the parents distraught, not knowing what happened to their child? The truth is that I had not physically stolen the child. I had merely disappeared.'

I was perplexed. What did she mean by that?

Another diary entry revealed it all.

I undertook the surrogacy for Parijat's operation. He was suffering from oesophageal cancer and needed surgery. It killed me to see him dying slowly before my eyes. I decided that if surrogacy could provide enough money for the operation, then that was what I would do.

But just as I underwent the gestational surrogacy, Parijat died. I had thought he had time. I was wrong. I had not told my mother-in-law about the surrogacy. She smiled when she saw my stomach begin to protrude. 'It will be a son,' she prophesied. 'Parijat reborn.'

People find consolation in such little things. 'Eat well,' she told me. 'Look after yourself. You have another life to take care of.'

She hovered around me all the time, almost smothering me with her attention. Then one day she absent-mindedly stepped in front of a moving bus and died. Her death depressed me, and I felt I had no reason to live. Just then, Mala kicked in my stomach for the very first time, and I found my reason to live. There was a child growing within me. It was not somebody else's child I was carrying in my womb. It was my child. It was Parijat reborn.

I packed my bags and left the city. I travelled from place to place until I reached Lonavala. I knew instinctively that this was where I would live. It is a small hill station near Pune, but I found peace here. There is so much beauty and serenity in Lonavala. I knew that if I started living here, I would heal.

No one knew me here, and no one would suspect the truth. For everyone I was Palash Sanyal, wife of late Parijat Sanyal, carrying his child.

Suvarna and Suyash must have been heartbroken by my disappearance. They would have tried to contact the police. But they would not have known if I was alive or dead. They may have thought I had taken my life in a fit of depression. Perhaps they believed I was one of the unclaimed bodies in the mortuary of a lesser-known city. How long could they search for me?

Mala is a grim reminder of what I did. Whenever I see her, I see Suvarna in her. Suvarna and Suyash had been overwhelmed when I agreed to be a surrogate. How heartbroken they must have been when I disappeared. Did they wonder what had happened to their child?

I stole their biological child from them—the one they had yearned for, the child Suvarna had hoped to hold in her arms one day. I wonder if they ever had the courage to try again. Did they go for another round of IVF? Did they find another surrogate? Or did they give up the dream of having their own child and decide *to adopt a child from an orphanage?*

They had so much love to give. Any child they brought home would have been lucky. It has been nearly nineteen years now, but I can never overcome the guilt I feel for what I did. I look over my shoulder constantly, wondering if I will be caught for stealing a baby.

Carrying Mala in my womb does not make me a mother, looking after her for nearly nineteen years probably does. Still, I am so afraid that when Mala learns the truth, she will end up hating me.

So, there it was—the plain, unvarnished truth. I was Suyash's daughter. The man I had blamed for my mother's death. Everything made sense now: Suyash's shock at seeing her after so many years, her fear of being arrested and jailed for stealing Suyash and Suvarna's biological child and her leap from Tiger Point to end it all.

I sat on the bed and sobbed.

Suddenly, I realized that I was not an orphan. I had a family. The thought began to excite me. I needed to meet Suyash and tell him that I had learnt the truth.

I boarded a bus to Pune and reached his house after a few hours. This time a servant opened the door. He was even more imposing than Suyash. I told him that I needed to see Suyash.

'Do you have some official work with him?' he asked.

Luckily for me, Suyash stepped out of the drawing room just then. I wanted to fling my arms around him. But the expression on his face made me stop.

'You again?' he said.

This was not the welcome I had hoped for.

'I am your daughter, aren't I?' I said without preamble.

'What makes you say that?' he asked, his voice cold.

'I found her diaries,' I said. 'They explained everything. The fear she carried, her glancing back constantly, her living in isolation. I realize now why we had no relatives or friends. Ma did not want the truth about my birth to come out.'

He remained silent.

'I am eighteen years old—the right age,' I continued. 'I know I am not adopted. I have even brought the birth certificate from the hospital where I was born.'

Still, he said nothing.

'We can do a DNA test to confirm paternity,' I added, desperation creeping into my voice.

Traumas like this either bring a family together or tear it apart. I began to feel afraid.

I had not seen Suvarna anywhere. Maybe they were divorced. Maybe he had remarried. Perhaps he had children of his own. Maybe I was an unwelcome intrusion in his perfect world.

Eighteen years is a long time. Long enough to forget someone. I did not even know if he had tried to find me.

'Say something,' I urged, willing him to speak.

'I don't need a DNA test,' he said at last.

He saw the confusion on my face.

'Come with me,' he said, leading me down the corridor to a room at the end. He flung open the door and my gaze landed on a painting on the wall.

Me! I thought, startled.

'Suvarna,' he informed me grimly. 'She had a nervous breakdown after Chhavi disappeared… After years of childlessness, we had found a surrogate. We treated Chhavi like a sister. We paid her handsomely—we knew she had only agreed to the surrogacy because she needed the money for Parijat's operation. Suvarna was longing to hold her child. Chhavi stole her dream from her—and along with it, her will to live.

'Suvarna could never recover from that betrayal. For months, she waited to hold you. And then, just as the time for the delivery approached, Chhavi vanished. We looked for her everywhere, but she had buried herself too deep.

'Three years later, Suvarna jumped from Tiger Point in Lonavala—from almost the spot Chhavi did. I go there every year to pay homage. More often now, since I have been posted here.'

'You never remarried?' I asked.

'If you had known Suvarna, you would know I could not. I could never find anyone like her.'

I looked at his face, my eyes searching. He looked so weary. There were many things I wanted to do—brush the hair from his forehead, make him a cup of tea, pour out my heart to him.

But all that could wait.

I ran into his arms and said, 'I'm home, Dad.'

He looked at me for a long moment, his expression unreadable. My heart sank. *Was I unwelcome in his home?*

He finally smiled and said, 'At last.'

2

The Dark Night

There is nothing like the desert to make one realize just how infinitesimal one really is. It stretches on endlessly. One can only see miles and miles of sand. The wind that blows into one's face bites into the skin. The silence screams.

I look at the sand dunes around me, seemingly identical, and feel bewildered. There is no habitation nearby.

Realization strikes me then: we are really and truly lost.

The sand swirls and flies into my eyes. They begin to burn.

'Papa, my eyes hurt,' Samrat shouts.

'Wear your sunglasses,' I say, pulling mine from my pocket. As I speak, more sand blows into my face. I tie a handkerchief around my mouth. Samrat follows suit and giggles.

'We look like bandits,' he says.

Samrat's voice is smooth, not gruff. Not yet.

'Papa.'

I turn back. *Now what?*

My twelve-year-old son is struggling to keep pace. He does not know how to walk in the desert. His feet sink into the sand.

'Take off your shoes—you will be able to walk better,' I advise.

It is the wrong advice. He does my bidding, flinching as the hot sand burns his feet; he tries to walk bravely but soon gives up and puts his shoes back on. Then he digs his feet deep into the sand and ploughs along again.

I look at him in despair. I will have to confess that we are lost.

It was foolhardy to come here without a guide. The desert is not for the weak-hearted. It is for bravehearts—those willing to face adversity and overcome it.

'Papa, I am thirsty,' Samrat murmurs, his voice faint. He is losing strength.

Suddenly I see someone floating towards us. It must be an apparition. It cannot be real.

As it comes closer, I realize that it is a man in a white kurta and dhoti, walking sure-footedly across the sand. There is a strange expression on his face. He must think our appearance to be frightening. He soon realizes we have handkerchiefs around our mouths for protection against the sand.

'Lost your way?' he asks. His voice is gruff, but his eyes are kind.

I nod.

'Looking for someone?' he asks.

I shake my head.

'My house is nearby; you can rest there. You can even spend the night,' he offers. 'Tomorrow, you can be on your way.' He then glances at the sky and says, 'It will be dark soon.'

I look at Samrat and sigh with gratitude. He could not have walked much longer. He needs to regain his strength.

'Our vehicle broke down,' I mumble as we follow him.

We seem to be miles from anywhere. After a while, his house comes into view. It is a long, single-storeyed building with a big courtyard. The whitewashed walls surrounding the house are adorned with beautiful murals. From a distance, they seem like Warli paintings—but that is only because I am familiar with Warli. This must be Rajasthani folk art.

Tied to a wooden stump, a little way off, is a camel. Samrat's eyes widen with intrigue. He has never seen a camel outside a zoo.

The man smiles indulgently. 'Don't go too close to the camel,' he warns Samrat. Then he turns to me and adds, 'My brother-in-law has come to fetch my wife; he is taking her to his house. The camel belongs to him.'

I bend my head slightly as I enter his house. Samrat walks in behind me. Big leather stools are scattered across the room. I sit on one and try to hide my grimace. The leather is stiff.

The man notices my expression and laughs gently. 'This is camel leather,' he explains.

He informs us that his name is Madho Singh before disappearing into the kitchen to speak to his wife.

I hear raised voices. He must be asking her to prepare something for us. She must be annoyed—especially as she was about to leave. Madho Singh sounds embarrassed.

After some time I hear footsteps receding. His wife has left with her brother. A little later, Madho Singh reappears with two glasses of buttermilk, which he places before Samrat and me. I grab mine and drink thirstily. I had not realized how dehydrated I was.

Madho Singh disappears into the kitchen again and returns with two thalis, each containing two bajra rotis, a large dollop of white butter and bowls of saag. I do not know what greens his wife has put into the saag, but it is delicious. After two rotis, I am sated. I glance at Samrat and smile. He has not spoken a word since we arrived, busy wolfing down the meal.

Madho Singh does not eat with us. He sits in the courtyard and eats there, respecting our privacy. He then calls us outside and begins to talk. There is a hookah by his side. Perhaps he has been craving company.

There is so much to talk about. It is funny how people sometimes willingly confide in strangers things they would not tell even their near and dear ones. There is a certain comfort in the anonymity such conversations offer. Strangers are, well, like ships that pass in the night. Madho Singh knows he will not see us again.

'I am a truck driver,' he tells me.

'Then why are you not on the road?' I ask.

'I haven't driven for the last three months. In fact, I have left my job.'

'What happened?' I ask gently.

'I was involved in an accident,' he says.

'Oh?'

'I was on the Delhi-Jaipur highway. It was the dead of night. A car was ahead of me. It was not speeding—I was. My truck hit the car. It jumped into the air and turned turtle. It was an accident. God knows it was an accident. But I did not stop. I drove away.'

I glance at Samrat. He is silent. Then, he stands up and starts walking away.

‘Were there any casualties?’ I ask, watching as my son disappears inside the house.

For a moment, Madho Singh is silent.

‘I read about it in the newspapers. The mother and daughter died. I should have stopped and taken them to the hospital. Maybe with timely medical aid, they would have survived. I should have gone to the police. But I was a coward. The guilt gnaws at me. I have not been able to drive since.’

I close my eyes. I remember the night so clearly.

Juhi, Samrat and Rumi and I were going to Ajmer for a holiday. A truck hit us from behind. I lost consciousness. When I woke up, I saw Samrat standing by the road, trying to flag down a passing vehicle. A kind-hearted man took us to the hospital. Everything else is a blur.

No one seemed to know who the driver was. But I hired the best detective I could find. He spoke to the officials, the truck drivers and the witnesses. Eventually, I found out who had hit us.

It was an accident, I tell myself. *He is repentant. Sending him to jail will not get Juhi or Rumi back.*

We had come looking for their killer and exact revenge. But we got lost—and the good Samaritan who rescued us has turned out to be the killer.

Can I forgive him?

I get up and walk towards the house. Samrat is there, with a hatchet in his hand—the one I had seen earlier, lying beside a pile of firewood near the kitchen door.

‘Papa,’ he says.

My eyes waver. I have come to like Madho Singh. I have accepted his hospitality. How can I take his life?

But Samrat’s face is implacable. He cannot forgive. He sees

my expression and asks, 'What about Mummy and Rumi?'

I know he will not be appeased till he gets justice—or revenge.

With leaden steps, I walk towards Madho Singh's charpai, the hatchet in my hand.

3

The Parcel

A pall of gloom hung over our house. Once, it had been full of laughter. The gloom was inevitable. I wondered if it would ever lift.

'Not until a miracle occurs,' I muttered to myself.

I never believed in miracles—until Garima walked into my life.

Garima.

I jerked my head suddenly. How could I have forgotten!

I put the glass of orange juice on a tray and took it to her. She sat in the drawing room, in an armchair, her legs stretched out. She was wearing a black and white kaftan. I wondered if her choice of colours was symbolic, as there were no colours left in her life any more.

'Garima, orange juice,' I said gaily. It took effort to bring animation into my voice.

She smiled serenely, her eyes still closed. 'You are so good to me, Ajay,' she said softly.

'Why wouldn't I be, my love? Nothing has changed,' I said.

'Everything has changed after the accident,' she said sadly.

'Don't say that.' I put my fingers on her lips, stopping her from saying more. Then I placed the glass in her hands. I knew she wanted to be alone with her thoughts—which, I suspected, were morbid. If I had been in her place, mine certainly would have been.

I stepped out of the room and almost collided with Anahita, Garima's elder sister. Once upon a time, I would have bristled at the sight of her—but not any more. The truth was that Garima needed her. No—if I were honest, I needed her too. Someone had to take care of Garima now, and who better than her own sister?

I returned to my study, sat down at the desk, and switched on my laptop.

The words swam before my eyes. I knew it was due to exhaustion. I had been having sleepless nights ever since Garima's accident. How could I have anticipated it?

Yes, I was the Superintendent of Police in a Naxal-infested district. I often received death threats. But that is part and parcel of a police officer's life. We learn to take threats in our stride.

I remember the day of the accident vividly.

It was my birthday. I woke up feeling good, whistling softly as I walked over to the dining table. Even though it was my birthday, I still had to work. I had planned to take Garima out for dinner to the only decent restaurant in town—The Oyster World. It was a multicuisine place that served the Chinese food Garima loved, and the Mediterranean I preferred.

Just when I was about to sit down for breakfast, Bahadur, our domestic help, entered the drawing room with a large parcel in his hands. It looked like a cake box.

Someone has sent me a birthday cake, I thought. *Who could it be?*

I had many well-wishers.

I called out to Anahita. She usually took care of all our mails and parcels.

Suddenly, Garima entered the room and rushed towards the parcel, as excited as a child.

'Don't, Garima, don't!' I shouted, as though seized by a premonition.

But Garima did not listen. She ripped open the parcel—and a bomb exploded.

'Ajay!' she screamed in pain as she collapsed. My world came to a standstill.

From then on, everything was a blur. I stood frozen in the dining room. It was Anahita who knelt beside Garima, even as she rang the hospital. The ambulance arrived fifteen minutes later. Garima was placed on a stretcher and taken to the district hospital, where the doctors were waiting.

They examined her for a long time while I sat outside, my face drenched in sweat, feeling helpless.

Would Garima survive?

I closed my eyes and prayed. When they finally delivered their verdict, my world went dark. The parcel bomb had taken away her sight.

The doctors assured me that her other injuries—the burns and the scars—would heal with time and surgery. But they gave me no hope for her eyes.

Garima was kept sedated for days. Her eyes were bandaged.

She looked like a battle-scarred warrior. I had never loved her more.

'It should have been me, it should have been me,' I repeated to myself. The bomb had been meant for me. I should have opened it. I was the intended victim. Not Garima.

'You never open parcels. I always do,' said Anahita when she heard me ranting.

I nodded my head. Anahita was the efficient one. Ever since she had moved in six months ago, she had taken over the household. Garima had been relieved. She had retreated into her world of oils and turpentine, canvases and easels. She had been planning her first exhibition.

'Those who sent the parcel did not know that,' I said.

A police officer has many enemies. 'What if it was the Naxalites?' I wondered aloud.

'Unlikely,' said Sumit, the Sub-Divisional Police Officer who had come home to see Garima. 'Why would they do that? Why not simply ambush your vehicle?'

I had to agree. 'It must have been an enemy of mine,' I said. I had many enemies.

∽

'Is there no hope?' I asked the doctor every time he visited Garima.

He would shake his head. 'I am afraid not. The injuries are too severe. Garima will never be able to see.'

I did not believe him, so I took her to the state hospital and then to the Dr Rajendra Prasad Ophthalmic Centre in New Delhi. At last, I had to accept it. Garima would never see again.

Two months after the accident, Garima asked me to resume work. 'Your leave is up. Your colleague has been living in the circuit house. How long will you sit at home and nurse me? I have Anahita to look after me.'

She was right of course. I had been away from work for too long.

I returned, ashamed by the fact that I was feeling relieved. Work provided me an escape—from a reality that was as bitter as it was daunting. Garima was blind. She would never be able to see. Both of us would have to live with this fact.

I should have known. I should have suspected.

Garima, who loved vibrant colours—reds and yellows, greens and blues—who painted so effortlessly on her canvases, celebrating life as it were, could not imagine a life without colour.

There have been blind musicians like Stevie Wonder and deaf musicians like Ludwig van Beethoven. But painters? They needed to see.

Garima could not imagine a world that was dark. So, she took an overdose of sleeping pills.

When I returned home from work, I found her asleep. I tried to wake her, but her hands were cold. I knew immediately that Garima was no more.

I tried to scream, but my voice failed. I ran out of the room blindly and almost cannoned into Anahita.

'What happened?' she asked. Seeing the tears streaming down my face, she understood.

Cremating Garima was the hardest thing I had ever done. I loved her to distraction.

The next evening, after the cremation, as I saw Anahita sitting in the drawing room, a wave of hatred surged through me. If I could have spanned her neck with my bare hands and killed her, I would have.

She was the one who was supposed to die.

The parcel bomb had been meant for her. It had seemed such a brilliant idea. A police officer is threatened so often—no one would have suspected the truth. Anahita always opened the mails. She was supposed to open that parcel, and poof, she would have gone—and with her, the threat to reveal our one-night stand to Garima.

How had it come to this? I still could not believe it.

Garima had gone to Delhi for the weekend to meet a friend. I had been at home, inebriated, and Anahita had been more than willing—no, she had been predatory. Later, she began making veiled threats, saying she would never leave Garima now.

The bomb had seemed the perfect solution. But it didn't go as planned.

Anahita was still alive. A possibility I had not contemplated.

Now Anahita and I only had each other.

I felt bile rise in my throat. I had failed once. But I would not fail again.

I owed it to Garima.

4

Maya

I had no premonition before opening the email that it would have a cataclysmic impact on my life. It was from someone called Joy, who lived in Florida.

He wrote: Hi, the most amazing thing has happened. I got my DNA tested from the site 23&Me and received the report just now. And guess what? The site, which tracks people with similar DNA, says we are a 50 per cent match. That means you are my brother. How is that possible? I am writing with great hope. Please respond to this email.

I read it with astonishment. Then I opened the report Joy had attached.

It was impossible. I was certain I was an only child. My mother died when I was twelve and had no siblings. Clearly, the report was incorrect. Apparently, even DNA tests could be wrong.

I closed my eyes as I recalled the day I had taken a DNA test. It was a year ago, when I had visited the US. My cousin Varun, who lives in New York, had insisted on it.

'Forewarned is forearmed,' he had said. 'Better to know what diseases you are at risk for as you grow older.'

I had cringed. I did not want to know. My father had developed Alzheimer's, and I was not ready to find out if I was likely to suffer the same fate. Sometimes ignorance is bliss, and I would have preferred to stay ignorant.

But Varun can be very persuasive. I was a guest in his home, and he offered to pay for the test—I could hardly refuse. And as he pointed out, all I had to do was to spit in a container. 'How difficult can that be?' he had teased. 'I remember, as a child, you were always drooling.

When I received the report, I was petrified. It flagged several markers for diseases I had not even considered. But I am a doctor—I knew those markers really meant nothing. I decided to forget the whole thing. And now this?

I slumped on the sofa, lost in thought. My memories of my mother had begun to fade. She had died nearly twenty years ago. My parents had parted ways—a fact I came to know much later.

Maya. That was my mother's name. I rolled it on my tongue. I loved the name. I loved my mother too.

She was an amazing woman—warm and empathetic, who brought joy wherever she went.

I shook my head. I was a doctor for God's sake, not a poet! But she really had been magic. She could turn anything into a work of art. Every birthday, she would give me a handmade gift, wrapped in the most amazing way. I had kept them all—the gifts and wrappers—and I am glad that I did. I was not a hoarder, but those were some of the few things I had left of her.

What could I possibly say to Joy? He sounded hopeful. It was clear he was adopted—how else could he make such an outrageous claim ? I could simply ignore the email. But he did not seem like someone who would give up easily. I was sure that if I ignored him for too long, he would bombard me with emails.

So, after a few days, I replied: As far as I know, I am an only child. My parents were separated. My mother died years ago. I suspect the DNA report is incorrect.

He responded immediately: That is unlikely. Do ask your father about this. Surely, he would know.

That entire day, I could not think of anything else. I kept telling myself I knew my family. I knew that I was an only child. My father and mother had separated when I was away at boarding school. I never really got to know what had gone wrong. I thought they had loved each other. It was my mother who had left my father. She died a year later.

I was brought up by my father, a taciturn and reclusive man. I spent my adolescence in boarding school, for which I was grateful. Left with him, I too might have turned morose and taciturn.

The next day was a Sunday. I dragged myself to the nursing home where Dad lived. It was a visit I hated. I dreaded the sight of Papa slumped in an armchair, drooling a little. I disliked the way his attendant looked at him with narrowed eyes and a barely disguised look of disgust. I hated going there every weekend to see Dad, with his mind in the grips of Alzheimer's. I loathed the thought that one day I too might get the disease.

I knew there was little point in posing the conundrum

before him. He would not know. He had his good days, but this did not seem like one of them. Still, a force beyond my comprehension compelled me.

'Hey, Papa,' I said after a while.

He turned and looked at me suspiciously.

'Milind,' I said, hoping to jog his memory. All I really wanted was to go home, sink into my lounger and pick up the book I had left open at page 47.

Visiting Papa every weekend was a weekly performance I was forced to make, because in India sons are expected to be dutiful. I was expected to look after my father. That I had abdicated my responsibility by putting him in a nursing home was already a black mark against me. Not that I cared.

I had stopped caring the day my mother left home, never to return. School had been my refuge. I did not want to come back home to a father who was melancholic, nervous and depressed. I was relieved when I cleared the medical entrance examinations after Class XII. It meant being away from home for another seven or eight years.

When I finally did return, the signs were already there—Papa's forgetfulness and his proclivity to lose things. Then came the day he could not locate the house he had lived in for thirty years.

The diagnosis was what I had feared: Alzheimer's.

I hired an attendant to look after him; it worked until the day we lost him again. He simply walked out of the front door and disappeared. The attendant was not really to blame. He had been on a loo break.

This time I got a call from the police station. A kind man had seen Papa wandering aimlessly five kilometres from our house. Seeing his neat clothes and blank expression, he had taken him to the nearest police station. Luckily, I'd had a bracelet made with Papa's name, our address and phone number just in case of such an eventuality. After that, I decided it was unsafe to keep him at home. He was better off under institutional care.

Fifteen minutes into my visit, I said, 'You know, Papa, I got an email from someone claiming to be my brother. He says that we share 50 per cent of our DNA. How is that possible?'

'So Maya was right,' Papa said suddenly.

Somewhere, through the fog of his disease, he had remembered my mother's name.

Then he burst into tears.

I was mystified. No, to be honest, I was dumbstruck. I had expected him to deny the whole thing. Instead, he rose from his armchair, walked slowly towards the almirah and took out a diary. He opened it and handed it to me.

Maya left our home today. I am glad she did. Her tears could not move me. Nor could her pleas. She said the child she was carrying was mine. I told her I had been abroad for a year and had returned less than four months ago. But it was clear she was about six months pregnant. Her abdomen had ballooned soon after she told me about the pregnancy. She could not be just two months pregnant, as she claimed.

Suddenly her eyes grew cold. 'You don't believe me, Mukul. You don't trust me,' she said quietly.

'No,' I shouted. 'You must have had an affair in my absence. I do not want to know who the father is. But you must abort the child.'

'No. Never,' she said.

'Then get out of the house,' I said in a rage.

I had not truly thought she would leave. After all, where could she go? She had been orphaned young. Her aunt, who had raised her, had died. She had no close family.

But Maya said, 'If there is no trust, there is no marriage.' She walked out, back straight, and never looked back.

I had expected the thought of Milind would hold her back, but he was away at boarding school.

After she left, I sat down in a daze. What had I done? Maya and I rarely fought. It was her presence that had given meaning to my life. Why did I let her go? Then a wave of anger swept through me. She was the guilty one. I was the one who had been betrayed. Why should I grieve? I was glad she had left. I did not try to find her. I wonder if she hoped I would.

I flipped through the diary and came across another entry written about eight months later:

I saw the obituary today. I would have missed it if I had not seen the newspaper. Nobody cared to inform me of Maya's death. I was devastated. As I drove to the cremation ground, I thought of the thirteen long years we had spent together—years filled with love and laughter. With Maya, I had learnt what happiness truly was.

When I reached the cremation ground, I saw Swapnil, my childhood friend, performing the last rites. A searing pain shot through me as I realized who had betrayed me. I now knew who the father of her unborn child was. I knew where Maya had gone after leaving me and where she had been all this while.

I felt nothing. Just a great emptiness. I was dead inside. Maya is now a forgotten chapter in my life. I wonder if I will ever be able to tell the truth about her to Milind.

I closed my eyes. Tears threatened to roll down my cheeks. It took great restraint to hold them back.

I remembered my mother. She smiled a lot and laughed often. If our house had once reverberated with joy, it was because of her.

From Joy's letter, it was clear that she had given birth to a child, and that child had been adopted. Papa had known nothing about it.

I realized I needed to trace Swapnil Uncle. I remembered him from my childhood days—a tall and handsome man with premature grey hair. He had kind eyes, and he too laughed a lot.

Finding him was not difficult. I got his address from one of Papa's old friends.

I hesitated at his doorstep. What could I possibly say after all these years? I was still fumbling for words when he opened the door.

'Milind? You have not changed at all!'

I smiled. I had been twelve the last time I saw him. I was almost thirty-two now. Perhaps he had a photographic memory—or maybe I had not changed much at all. Perhaps I had always been quiet and solemn, just like my father.

I did not waste time with small talk. Swapnil Uncle must have suspected there was a purpose for my visit. People do not saunter into an old acquaintance's house after twenty years just to make a social call.

'I was just Maya's friend,' he said. Then he checked himself. 'No, I was Maya's rakhi brother. Mukul knew that. No outsider can destroy a marriage. Mukul did it to himself. Maya was just two months pregnant when he threw her out. There are cases where a woman's abdomen balloons early in pregnancy and makes it look as though she is six months pregnant.'

‘I know, I am a doctor,’ I said quietly.

He sighed. ‘Maya came to me because she had nowhere else to go. After childbirth, she had postpartum complications and died soon after delivery. I was a bachelor—she knew I would not be able to raise a child alone.

‘“Give him up for adoption,” she told me just before she died. “Who knows, he may get more love from them than he ever could from his own parents.”’

‘Mukul should have been there for Maya, but he was warped in his judgement. I performed the cremation, and later gave up the baby for adoption. It was the hardest thing I’ve ever done. I was tempted to keep him, but I knew Maya was right. I couldn’t do it alone. I’m so glad Joy found a loving home.’

After returning from Swapnil Uncle’s house, I emailed Joy and told him the whole sordid story: Yes, we are brothers, but you are the lucky one. Your adoptive parents gave you an abundance of love, while my mother died when I was twelve and my father is now suffering from Alzheimer's.

I forgot that my parents were Joy’s parents too!

I didn’t hear from him again. I was both relieved and disappointed—relieved that we now both knew the truth, and disappointed that he didn’t want to stay in touch.

Two months later, there was a knock at my door.

I recognized him the moment I opened it.

Joy looked just like our mother.

We stood facing each other awkwardly for a moment and then we hugged.

I looked at his parents, Jane and Dan Myers, who stood behind him. I knew instantly: Joy was indeed lucky. He had a loving home and devoted parents who had travelled halfway across the world so their son could meet his birth family.

I showed him our family album, and shared all the memories of my mother that I had tucked away in the recesses of my mind—memories I had never spoken aloud, because I knew they would hurt my father.

I took Joy and his parents to the nursing home to meet Papa.

Papa stared at Joy for a few minutes, expressionless. And then, sounding wonderstruck, he whispered: 'Maya. Oh, Maya.'

He hugged Joy and wept.

I joined them, and together we cried—for our mother, for the terrible misunderstanding between our parents, for our lost childhoods, and for all that might have been.

5

Father and Son

'Daddy,' asked Rohit, 'how did Mummy die?'

I looked up from the newspaper, startled. He stood before me, belligerent, his jaw set. He was in no mood for fairy tales.

'You know. I told you before—she died in an accident.'

'Lies. All lies,' he said, his stance aggressive. He waved a newspaper at me. It was old and yellowed, with its edges frayed.

How did he get hold of it? I wondered. I had hidden the newspaper cuttings in an old trunk, right at the bottom, beneath a thick blanket.

Meena. I swore under my breath.

The new maid, with her fetish for cleanliness. Every morning she stood outside my door, eyes reproachful. '*Babuji, phir se*, sir, again?' she would say, as though dropping a towel on the bathroom floor was a mortal sin. She must have taken out the old clothes to air them and dumped the newspapers on the balcony, where Rohit found them.

'I would have told you but…'

'I was too young,' he finished for me, his voice accusatory.

I flushed. 'I am sorry,' I stuttered.

'Sorry?' he sounded incredulous. 'She committed suicide. Did you drive her to it?'

I sighed. He must have read only an excerpt. He did not know the whole story. Thank God.

He stormed into his room and slammed the door. I heard the bolt click. He had locked himself in. I got up unsteadily. Dengue had left me weak. My joints ached. I tottered back to bed.

What was done was done.

Rohit refused to come out, even after Meena banged on the door three times. I began to panic. I hoped he hadn't done anything foolish.

Later, I felt feverish and delirious. Meena had left by then. I hadn't eaten—I was too nervous. Suddenly I heard movement. My sixteen-year-old son stood before me with a bowl of *khichdi* in his hands.

'Open your mouth,' he said, just as Anjali had said when I was ill with typhoid. 'Eat.'

I ate slowly. I didn't have the strength to eat quickly. Rohit spooned the food into my mouth, as patiently as a mother feeding a child. His eyes were brimming.

'How could she do that to you? How could she betray you?' he asked quietly.

It was clear he had read everything. He knew the full story. I had nothing more to add.

'She committed suicide. She hanged herself from the fan in a hotel room. Just a day before my birthday. While her lover went for a swim.'

His voice was bitter with disgust.

'Don't judge your mother too harshly. Society has judged her enough,' I said.

The newspapers, initially sympathetic, had turned voyeuristic, revelling in the scandal of a seemingly happily married woman found hanging in a hotel room; hotel records revealed she was not with her husband, but her lover.

Newspapers loved to bay for blood. Staid, boring husbands did not make headlines or boost newspaper sales. Illicit love affairs did. Especially when the man involved was someone like Mahesh Dadlani—high-profile, flamboyant—the media loved him.

Anjali and he had been having an affair for three years—while I wore blinders. The cuckolded husband. That was me. The press loved it. They dug up every detail—when they met, how long it had lasted, and more.

As the facts emerged, everything made sense. I finally understood why Anjali had gone to Mumbai so often. Not because she had to attend meetings, seminars, workshops, or consultations for her ad campaign. She was in a relationship with Mahesh Dadlani—the media czar.

Three years was a long time. How could I have been so blind?

'Do you want a DNA test done?' a reporter had once asked during an interview.

'No,' I'd said vehemently.

'Why didn't you get the DNA test done as the man had suggested?' Rohit asked me. 'It could have strengthened the case against Mahesh Dadlani. He might have been arrested for abetment to suicide.'

He was waiting for an answer, visibly disappointed when I said nothing.

I remembered telling the press and the police: 'He is my son, and he has been my son since the day he was born. Paternity does not matter to me.'

I thought of Anjali. For whom Rohit was not enough. Nor was our marriage. She had to seek pleasure elsewhere.

For a senior marketing manager in a leading firm, a university lecturer was, perhaps, too boring. She wanted more. I should have seen it, but I was so happy when Rohit was born that I overlooked it all. When she wanted to go to Mumbai just four months after his birth, I had voiced my reservations. But she had been persuasive and I gave in.

'Mrinal, you can manage,' she said, smiling. 'You make a better mother than I do.'

She wasn't wrong. I was the one getting up at night to change nappies. I was the one who crooned lullabies to Rohit so that Anjali could get her beauty sleep. I fed Rohit Cerelac.

But that was just the beginning.

The trips became more frequent. Anjali stayed away more often. I juggled my lectures and a baby.

Then, during a class, I got the call that changed everything.

'Are you Mrinal Sharma?' asked a disembodied voice.

'Yes,' I replied, not knowing the next few words would destroy my life. Rather, I felt annoyed at being disturbed in the middle of my lecture.

'I am sorry,' the man began. 'Your wife is dead.'

I recoiled. 'What happened? Was it a car crash?' I asked, numb and unable to react to the news.

Anjali was a rash driver. I suspected she had had a head-on collision with a truck. But the truth was far more sordid.

Why had Anjali committed suicide? I had no answers then. I am not much wiser now either.

Did Mahesh refuse to leave his wife and marry her? Did they have a fight? Or did guilt finally besiege Anjali? Had she been tottering on the brink of a nervous breakdown?

She was supposed to return the next day—for Rohit's first birthday. We had planned a quiet celebration. I was not someone she liked to flaunt. I did not blame her.

I blamed arranged marriages, which matched horoscopes, not personalities, where a groom who asked for no dowry was seen as a gift from heaven. I blamed my own arranged marriage, where Anjali's parents saw my PhD as something to be flaunted and ignored my plain, nondescript face.

We were a mismatched couple. I admitted that. Anjali was drawn to Mahesh because of his magnetic personality and the power he exuded. I paled in comparison.

I did not need three guesses to know who Rohit's biological father was. But Mahesh was not there when Anjali's contractions began. I was. He did not pace up and down the hospital corridor when she was rushed to the labour room. I did. He did not hold Rohit in his arms after he was born. I did. He did not see Rohit cut his first tooth. I did. He did not hear Rohit say 'Papa' before 'Mama.' I did.

Surely that counted for something. Surely *this* was how a father and son form a bond. Surely I had a stronger claim as Rohit's father than Mahesh.

'After Anjali left, I had nobody but you. I could not let them take you away from me,' I told him. 'You are my son and always will be. For me, paternity is a matter of faith.'

As I held Rohit tight, I thought I could still smell Johnson's baby powder on him. I knew it was just my imagination, but I also knew that no matter how tall he grew, he would always remain my baby.

Thankfully Rohit did not broach the subject ever again. Nor did he show any inclination to learn more about Mahesh Dadlani, who he must have suspected was his biological father.

It has been ten years since Rohit confronted me. Things have changed since then. He now works in Kolkata. I have become ill. I have liver cirrhosis.

I do not drink or smoke. Mine is non-alcoholic fatty liver disease. Something had to give way after Anjali's death. My health did. I am on my deathbed now—at least I think so. Maybe I am just depressed.

I need a liver transplant. But where will I find a donor? My brother volunteered, but he was not a match.

Government rules are so strict. And dead donors are rare. There is not enough awareness about organ donation in the country. I am reconciled to dying.

My doctor is hopeful of finding an altruistic donor, but I am not. I am a pessimist by nature—or maybe, over the years, I have become one.

It is difficult to live with betrayal. It leads to a sense of inadequacy.

The doctor rings me, asking me to come in for a check-up. He greets me enthusiastically when I arrive, his eyes shining.

'I have found a donor for you,' he says.

I am overwhelmed by God's kindness. Illness turns every non-believer into a convert. I was already a theist to begin with. Just then, someone enters the room.

It is Rohit.

My joy turns to dismay when the doctor says, 'Your donor.'

My face blanches. 'No, not Rohit,' I say.

'Why not? He is a match,' the doctor replies.

'He is too young. There may be complications. Something

may go wrong. There is a possibility he may die.'

'The liver is a remarkable organ; it regenerates,' the doctor insists.

Rohit says nothing. Just smiles broadly. He is perhaps happy that I will live a few more years because of him.

'Thank you, Rohit, for offering to give me a new lease of life,' I tell him.

He does not respond. I am slightly hurt. I expected him to say something.

But Rohit has more important things on his mind. He hands me two documents. They are DNA reports.

When did he take my sample? I do not remember, but then I had undergone a flurry of tests. I scan the reports. Rohit's and mine.

A 50 per cent match.

Is that possible? Is he really my son?

He envelops me in a bear hug. 'You're welcome, Papa,' he says.

6

The Amish Quilt

There are times when I think I can hear silence speak. I hear it whisper in the rustling leaves. I hear it just before the birds begin to chirp in the sky. I hear it when the night is still young.

This was one such moment.

Silence echoed through the woods, which stood on either side of the narrow road down which Rita drove at a leisurely pace. The branches bent low and brushed against the car windows as we passed. I was glad I had shut them.

'Look,' said Rita suddenly, and I raised my eyes to see a glorious sunset. Shades of crimson, orange and purple streaked the sky. Clouds criss-crossed through it. Perhaps it was my imagination, but I thought I could see hazy images inside the clouds. There was something surreal about the scene. The sky looked like a Salvador Dalí painting come alive.

The car moved ahead, and suddenly we emerged into

an open field. Beyond it, we saw buildings and houses. Up ahead, women dressed in black skirts, white blouses, aprons and bonnets were walking along the road. They reminded me of nuns going to chapel. The men beside them wore black trousers and white shirts. *Like penguins*, I thought, smiling to myself.

Then I heard the clip-clop of hooves. A horse-drawn carriage emerged from a lane and passed us. I caught my breath.

A horse-drawn carriage in the US in 2015?

I pinched myself.

'This is just for tourists, isn't it?' I asked tentatively.

'You are in Amish country, my friend,' Rita said, chuckling. 'You have no idea how the Amish live. They generate their own electricity, believe in vocational skills over formal education, are peace-loving—and they make some of the most beautiful artefacts in the world.'

'I didn't know. I haven't been in the US long enough,' I admitted.

She parked the car in a lane and we began walking towards a cluster of shops.

'Wild horses would not have dragged me to Amish country, but my sister Renee asked me for an Amish quilt for her birthday,' I said.

Rita raised her eyebrows. 'A quilt? I thought India had a hot climate,' she remarked.

'I thought so too, but you know sisters,' I commented.

'I didn't know you had one, Jay,' Rita frowned. 'You have never mentioned her.'

'I guess the subject never came up,' I murmured. After all, I had met Rita just three months earlier. I was doing a master's course in Chemistry at the University of Illinois, Urbana-Champaign.

'It's her birthday today,' I then blurted out.

'Then we must celebrate,' said Rita. 'Let us buy a cake,' she added.

I wondered where we could buy a cake in Amish country, but she suddenly entered a half-open door. I had no choice but to follow.

I found myself in a large hall. The aisles were stocked with food. The air was thick with the scent of apple pie, banana loaves and cinnamon buns. I inhaled deeply. It reminded me of home—the wholesomeness of home cooking.

Rita picked up a basket and filled it with two banana loaves, a chocolate cake, buns, some homemade cheese, and freshly ground spices. I imagined her later, curled up in her living room, music playing, nibbling cheese and sipping wine.

Suddenly her pace quickened.

'Let's head to the handicraft shops. It's getting late,' she said.

We marched towards a row of shops displaying handicrafts. I stopped short in front of the first window.

A quilt.

It was a patchwork quilt in mauve and pink, blue and purple, lilac and peach. The pattern was so intricate I stood spellbound. I knew instantly that this was the kind of quilt Renee would have loved.

I stepped into the shop. Rita followed.

'Is there something you wanted to buy?' asked a girl behind the counter, her head bent over a ledger. She sounded slightly impatient. It was nearly closing time and I realized that she must be getting ready to leave.

'A quilt. A handmade quilt,' I said.

'All our quilts are handmade,' she replied briskly. Then she looked up.

I gaped, gripping the counter for support.

It was—no, it couldn't be—Renee.

I must be hallucinating.

'What kind of quilt?' she asked.

'The best,' I said, trying to steady my voice.

'The one on display is the best we have. I made it myself,' she said proudly.

I did not ask to see others. I had fallen in love with the quilt the moment I saw it.

She packed the quilt carefully into a bag. I paid in cash. I glanced at the name pinned to her dress: Lucy.

It suited her.

As we were about to leave, I turned back.

'I have a request,' I said.

She looked surprised. Her expression turned to alarm when I added, 'May I take your photograph?'

As her eyes widened in dismay, Rita caught my hand in warning and pressed a flier into it. It stated clearly that the Amish valued their privacy. Tourists must not take photographs.

Two men stepped in from the back—perhaps Lucy's brothers.

'Is there a problem?' one of them asked.

I looked at the two men. They were taller than me, bearded, and burly. Although Rita had said the Amish were peace-loving, I suddenly felt threatened.

'You misunderstand,' I said quickly, fumbling in my wallet. I pulled out Renee's photograph and held it out.

'My sister, Renee.'

Lucy was the first to see it. She stared. 'Oh my God. It's true. She's my doppelgänger. I never believed in doppelgängers—but now I do. We look alike. We could be twins.'

I looked away, trying to hide the tears that threatened to spill. Rita held my hand firmly.

'Let's go. I told you—no photographs,' she whispered.

We had reached the door when Lucy called out, 'Sometimes we make exceptions.'

I turned around. She was smiling. So were the men.

I clicked her photograph.

'When did she die?' Lucy asked just as I was leaving.

'How did you know?' I whispered.

'No man carries a photo of his sister in his wallet without a reason. And no grown man cries without cause.'

I told her, haltingly, about that fateful day the year before. I'd taken Renee out to buy her birthday present. The car hit a divider and overturned. Renee, her face bloodied and bruised, died instantly.

I, who was at the wheel, walked away without a scratch.

I did not tell Lucy—but she understood. She saw the guilt that lived in me. Coming to Urbana-Champaign from New Delhi had been my way of escaping, but Renee continued to haunt my thoughts.

'When I saw your sister's photo, I felt an instant connection with her,' Lucy said.

I wondered if she said that to please me—or if she truly believed it.

'Come here whenever you miss your sister,' she added, as I waved goodbye.

We drove back in silence.

Then I told Rita, 'Renee died a year ago. Last night I dreamt of her. She asked me to buy her an Amish quilt.'

'I think she wanted you to meet Lucy—and remind you that though she may be gone, you still have to go on with the business of living,' said Rita gently.

I nodded. Maybe Rita was right. Maybe Renee wanted me to expunge my guilt and begin living again.

I knew that whenever the longing to see Renee became unbearable, I would visit that shop and speak to Lucy. Perhaps buy another quilt. Perhaps be comforted.

Perhaps Renee's ghost would stop haunting me.

Perhaps not.

Only time would tell.

7

Redemption

One's actions today determine one's tomorrows. That is what my mother believed.

Amma.

As I thought of her, guilt gnawed at me and chipped away at my composure. Grief was like a corrosive acid I seemed to have swallowed accidentally, which was now eating away at my insides. I simply could not get out of my mind the image of my mother hooked to a ventilator, her eyes fixed on the door, waiting for me to walk in.

I tried—really tried. But I could not forget the fact that I had been celebrating New Year's Eve with my girlfriend Anamika, my mobile switched off, when my cousin Randeep sent me a message saying Amma had been admitted to hospital for low sodium. It did not sound serious to me, even though he insisted I should come immediately.

But Randeep and I lived in different worlds. I was an

investment banker in New York; he was a lecturer in Delhi. I saw myself as stoic and worldly. He, I thought, panicked easily. Why couldn't he handle what I assumed was a minor ailment? I may have been a whiz with numbers, but I had no idea that low sodium could be fatal.

Still, I booked my tickets. I reached Delhi four days after receiving the message.

When I arrived at Max Saket Super Speciality Hospital, I learnt that Amma was gone.

A gut-wrenching pain hit me at the thought of Amma lying alone in that hospital, eyes on the door, waiting for her only son. I had never imagined she would die at fifty-nine. I had not thought her condition had become life-threatening. I did not even know what had triggered it.

I had failed her. I had betrayed my widowed mother, the woman who had been my emotional anchor. I was hedonistic; I berated myself. But remorse wouldn't bring Amma back.

I went through the cremation in a zombie-like state. Two days later, I hired a jeep and left for Haridwar to immerse her ashes in the Ganges.

I could have taken Randeep, or another cousin with me. Amma had lived in a joint family, unwilling to leave our ancestral home to join me in New York. And frankly, I'd been thankful—my studio apartment was no place for her. But now, I could not bear the thought of Randeep's accusing eyes or the silent condemnation of the others, who had already judged me guilty of neglect.

I carried the urn tightly, as though it contained the most precious thing in the world—because, of course, it did. It held the mortal remains of my mother.

At Har ki Pauri, I found a priest who began bargaining

about his fee. I couldn't have cared less. Five thousand rupees to perform the rites didn't seem excessive. I had no idea what the going rate was.

He took me into the river in a boat, chanted mantras and performed the puja while I released Amma's ashes into the Ganges. I closed my eyes, hoping to purge my guilt.

On a whim, I decided to stay the night in Haridwar instead of returning to Delhi.

What is it about religious places that grows on one? I wondered. Was it the languid pace of life or the presence of saffron-robed mendicants everywhere? Or was it simply the weight of guilt within me, which needed to be assuaged?

It did not matter. It gave me a day away from the prying eyes of my relatives before I returned to New York.

I chose a dharamshala at random, and then wondered if I would be able to survive a day in it. I was too fond of creature comforts. I was, in Anamika's words, a philistine. Perhaps, subconsciously, my stay in Haridwar was a form of penance.

That's when I saw her—walking towards me.

It could not be Amma. I had cremated her myself.

But from a distance, it looked like her: clad in a white saree, her face clear of any adornments. Was I delusional? Hallucinating? Was it Amma's ghost, coming for one last glimpse?

I tried to call out, but my throat was dry. I couldn't move.

As she came closer, I realized she was at least a decade younger. Just a middle-aged widow who looked very much like my mother.

The dharamshala I had chosen was clean but sparsely furnished. Dinner was about to be served. I felt a twinge of guilt admitting to myself that I was ravenous. Should I be this hungry while grieving?

But hunger, I realized, has little to do with grief.

The food—pooris, potato curry, pumpkin and boondi raita—could have rivalled a Michelin-starred meal. Or perhaps I was just that hungry.

That night, I wandered outside and sat on a bench in the park.

The woman I had mistaken for Amma came and sat beside me. I looked at her curiously, but she glanced away. It became clear she hadn't sought my company—she'd only chosen the bench because no other was free.

We sat in silence for a long time. And then I spoke.

I told her she reminded me of my mother, who had died three days ago. That I grieved not being able to see her before she died.

She too had a story to tell.

'It takes just a minute for life to fall apart. Mine shattered the day my husband, Girish, died. And he chose Karva Chauth to leave me.

'Like most married women in India, I had kept a fast for his long life. He was watching the television when he began to cough. I went to get him water. When I returned, he had collapsed on the sofa. I called the doctor, rushed him to hospital. They pronounced him dead.

'I worked hard to raise our eight-year-old son. But when he turned eighteen, he ran away—stealing all my jewellery and cash. Left me destitute.'

Her story shook me. I could imagine the struggles she had endured.

It offered little comfort to know her son was worse than me. That would not have consoled Amma, who, Randeep told me, had been pining for me until her final breath.

I swallowed the guilt rising in my throat.

The next evening, while settling my bill with the desk clerk, I saw her again.

'I didn't know you were staying here,' I began, but she didn't acknowledge me and disappeared inside.

'Do you know her?' the clerk asked curiously.

'I met her yesterday. We got talking. Hers is a very sad story. She was betrayed by her own son.'

'Her son?' he raised his eyebrows.

'The one who deserted her after stealing her jewellery and cash,' I said.

He said, 'Well, I had heard that she ran off with a man—probably a married one, though she did not know it at the time—who later deserted her. Her family refused to take her back.'

Saying that, he laughed raucously.

I felt a wave of anger rise against the clerk. He had no right to take pleasure in her misfortune. Then I began to feel sorry for the woman.

'Her son? Well, that is a new one,' said the clerk thoughtfully, unaware of my growing anger. I wondered if she had made up the story instead of telling me the sordid truth. If so, she was a skilled storyteller. But I did not blame her. Everyone yearns for a cloak of respectability. So did she.

'Which room is she staying in?' I asked, thinking I would leave some money for her.

He laughed. 'She cannot afford a room.'

'Not even in a dharamshala?' I asked.

He smiled. 'Not even here. She works in the kitchen and sleeps there at night. After all, how much space does she need?'

'How much is she paid?'

'Paid?' He raised his eyebrows again. 'Two thousand rupees.'

'What?' I exclaimed.

'She gets free food and a place to sleep as well—and this isn't a hotel, it's a charitable dharamshala,' he said defensively.

Two thousand rupees. That was what one tipped in a five-star hotel after a lavish meal. But this was not a hotel, as the clerk was so keen to clarify. No one left tips for her. Two thousand rupees a month to meet all her needs?

How did she survive?

I imagined her eyes lingering on a much-coveted saree in a shop window, and then quelling her longing. I imagined her standing near a kiosk, wanting to try something new, and then reminding herself she had to save for her old age.

What would happen to her when she grew older and could no longer work? If she were lucky, she might be sent to an old-age home. I imagined her, aged and helpless, at the mercy of indifferent caregivers—or worse, shivering on a pavement on a cold winter's night.

If she had a little money, she could have rented a room here. Perhaps she could have taken up work in a shop that paid better.

She was not my mother.

So what?

She was somebody's mother. And even if she was not, she could have been.

'How much does it cost to live here?' I asked the clerk.

He looked at me curiously and mentioned an amount for board and lodging. It was modest—less than sixty thousand rupees a year.

'I'll write a cheque,' I said.

I noticed a flicker of doubt cross his face. Perhaps he thought the cheque would bounce.

I stepped out and withdrew the money from a nearby ATM. Thankfully, I had more than one debit card.

'This is for her board and lodging for the entire year. I'll keep sending you the money annually,' I said upon my return.

He accepted the cash, then pointed to a sign on his desk. 'You need not have bothered to get the cash. We accept online payments too,' he said.

I was surprised. I did not think India had truly become digital.

I realized I could pay for ten years in advance. I did so and handed him my business card.

'Let me know when the rates change, and I'll transfer the additional amount,' I said.

He looked embarrassed. 'Don't worry. What you've paid should cover future increases.'

I then asked him to call her.

When she arrived, I handed her the receipt.

'Amma, you now have a room of your own, and your meals are taken care of for the next ten years. You may wish to keep working in the kitchen for a better income—or seek other work.'

Her eyes lit up. In that moment, her whole face changed. I saw tears she hadn't yet shed. They gave her eyes a strange luminescence.

Looking at her radiant face, I realized she must have been very beautiful in her youth.

She gripped the edge of the table for support and whispered, 'No one has ever been this kind to me.'

She clearly knew the value of what she'd been given.

'You must love your mother very much,' she added. She was perceptive.

Then she said, 'Wait a moment—I'll be back.'

She returned holding something in her hands. 'This is for you,' she said, handing me a scroll.

I unrolled it. It was a Madhubani painting of Radha and Krishna.

It was exquisite. The colours leapt off the paper—vibrant and alive.

'I made it myself,' she said with pride. 'This is what I love to do. And now that you've gifted me peace of mind, this is what I want to continue doing.'

'I shall frame it and hang it in my room,' I said. And I meant it. She had talent—an abundance of it, in fact. All she needed was support, just a little handholding.

'You have done for me what my own son didn't,' she said.

The desk clerk looked startled.

So it was true, he realized—she *did* have a son.

'You have provided for me as if I were your own mother. May God bless you. This gesture of yours will change my life,' she said.

I smiled at her and then realized that it was a life-changing moment for me too.

It was time to give back.

I was thirty-five. I had made my money as an investment banker. I could, with Anamika, start a trust in Amma's name and provide support to destitute women in Haridwar and Rishikesh. We could help them develop vocational skills and find outlets for their products.

I could do this even while based in New York. One could always find partners in India.

Maybe even Randeep.

Perhaps that way—I could finally earn redemption.

8

Second Honeymoon

Memories have a strange way of intruding into one's present. You cannot shut them out easily. I try. I try very hard. Prateek has gone out of his way to make our second trip to Italy comfortable. According to him, it is our second honeymoon. He tries to ensure that old memories do not intrude. We are travelling business class this time. 'I encashed my air miles,' he says. But he cannot meet my eyes. We do not travel so often. How did he collect so many air miles?

After the check-in, we head towards the Air India lounge. Prateek is as excited as a child. 'What will you have?' he asks.

'Soup and bread,' I say.

He makes a face. 'We are celebrating ten years of togetherness—try something else,' he says, eyeing the sumptuous fare laid out.

'Well, if we want to spend the next forty years together, we must be careful,' I respond.

He laughs.

We board the plane two hours later, and I sink into the plush business class seat. I close my eyes and hear the air hostess murmur, 'Coconut water or strawberry smoothie?' I choose coconut water.

The hostess smiles, passes me my drink and moves ahead.

Prateek sinks into the seat beside me. I hear the rustle of a newspaper. 'Your name is in the papers,' he says.

Ten years ago, it had been my photograph.

I have a sense of déjà vu. The years roll back as I recall our first trip.

We are travelling to Italy. Economy class. Prateek says that he has collected enough air miles to buy us free tickets. He must have been collecting them for ages. We will stay for four days with his aunt in Rome. That is how two people, very much in love but without much money, are beginning their life together. I smile.

It is our honeymoon, but I would rather stay with his aunt in Rome than in a hotel in Nainital or Mussoorie. Hotels are expensive, and if we had to stay in hotels for the entire duration, we would become broke. Anyway, I like Leela Mausi. She is a good sort. Besides, we will stay in a hotel for four days in Venice, the most romantic destination in the world.

I look around the cabin curiously. Prateek looks apologetic. He has not been able to get the first-row seats in economy, where there are only two seats on each side. That row has gone to a couple with a child. Prateek has managed to get an aisle and a middle seat in the second row.

'It doesn't matter,' I say with a smile, 'I am taking the aisle seat.'

He groans. He hates the idea of being squashed between two passengers.

I secretly wish I had a window seat. I could then see the plane fly above the clouds and enjoy the morning sun filtering through the window. This way, I will share my husband with a stranger.

A woman with a baby comes and sits next to Prateek. I shudder. Just how many babies are there on this flight? I am a doctor—a paediatrician by profession. I love children, but I hate them bawling.

'A newborn's cry is the most beautiful sound in the world.' How many times have I heard that? But I can vouch for the fact that when a baby's wailing wakes you up night after night, the fascination wanes.

The plane is about to take off when our neighbour's baby begins to cry. It has a shrill, high-pitched voice, like the screeching siren of an ambulance—or the fire brigade. Of course, I exaggerate. But this is my honeymoon, and I had yearned for a little privacy. I hope the woman will be able to quieten the baby. But it is in vain. The infant's cries reach a crescendo.

The air hostess comes with a tray of cotton wool and candy. I quickly grab both and stuff my ears with cotton. The baby's cries abate somewhat. Then I begin to suck the sweet. The baby begins crying again.

'Why don't you put some cotton wool in your child's ears? It will lessen the earache,' I tell the mother.

She looks at me suspiciously.

'I am a doctor—the cotton wool will drown the noise of the engine,' I tell her reassuringly.

She looks sceptical but decides to give it a try. The child's cries cease. I heave a sigh of relief. Maybe I will be able to sleep after all.

However, sleep continues to elude me. I grab a newspaper.

It is yesterday's. The morning edition is not yet out at 5 a.m. But I have not read this one either—I was too busy packing. The headlines are about GDP and the forthcoming elections. I skim over them. Politics bores me, as does economics. I like human interest stories.

At the bottom of the front page, I read a news item and get goosebumps. The headline reads 'Child Snatching' and there is a photo of a month-old baby who has been stolen from his pram while his mother was talking to a friend in the park.

'How could she be so careless?' I think. I look at the devastated woman's face. Her eyes look smudged with kajal. The baby has the gentlest face. All babies look alike, I have always said. But baby Anmol is adorable. Perhaps it is his dimpled chin, or the mole on his cheek, which the photograph has captured so clearly. I want to croon to him. To sing lullabies. 'How can anyone take a month-old baby away from his mother?' I wonder angrily. I pray that she gets Anmol back.

I fold the newspaper and begin fiddling with the knobs of the in-flight entertainment. Prateek leans over and helps me. I settle down to watch an old English classic—*Casablanca*. I have seen it before, but I want to see it again. I loved Humphrey Bogart in the film. I look tenderly at Prateek. Our love story is not as dramatic as Ingrid Bergman and Humphrey Bogart's, but it is dramatic enough.

'How did a doctor and an engineer get married?' Just how many times have we been asked that!

Prateek loves to tell the tale. 'The first time we met, we spent the night together,' he would say dramatically. Then he would pause and add, 'On a Ferris wheel.' He loves the look of surprise on our friends' faces. It could figure in the column 'Strange but True'.

I can never forget the night I had gone to see the Nauchandi Mela in Meerut, trying to relive old childhood memories. I had a sudden yearning to get on the Ferris wheel. I was alone, so the man at the gate bundled me into a seat with the next person in the queue. Prateek and I sat as far apart as possible. I felt a sense of breathless excitement as we went up. I recalled that coming down was worse. My aunt had once advised me, 'Just hold your breath, and expel it slowly as you come down.' It worked. The empty feeling in the pit of my stomach abated.

Then the Ferris wheel stopped halfway. I looked in horror at the man next to me.

'Don't blame me, I had nothing to do with it,' he said quickly.

'I know that,' I said angrily. 'I want to know what will happen now.'

'Let us wait and watch. They will have to get us out—we cannot be stranded here all night,' he said.

However, we remained sitting there for hours.

'I am hungry,' I said after a couple of hours. 'I need something to eat.'

'You are carrying such a large purse, maybe there's something inside.'

I rummaged through it and found a packet of Britannia Marie biscuits. 'I'll survive,' I said airily, and began eating them hungrily. Halfway through I felt guilty and offered him one.

'I wish you hadn't,' he said, taking it. Then he grinned sheepishly and took out a large bar of Cadbury Fruit & Nut from his pocket. 'Have some,' he said, somewhat reluctantly.

We spent the entire night talking. The Ferris wheel was repaired only at six in the morning. However, Prateek insists that I dozed off after midnight, and since I had rested my head on his shoulder, he had not been able to sleep a wink.

It took him a year to win me over. I loved my own love story.

The baby next to Prateek starts howling again. I look at the mother seated in the front row, who is holding her baby under a blanket. He has not stirred even once.

'What a placid child,' I say with a chuckle. 'I would not mind having a baby like that.'

I blush.

We are on our honeymoon and I have already begun planning a family. In fact, I have even chosen the children's names: Arnav and Akanksha. I believe in being prepared.

The mother in the front row has her eyes closed. *Did she give the baby Benadryl?* I wonder, even as I turn on the in-flight entertainment once again. I begin to watch *U Me Aur Hum*. I love Kajol and Ajay Devgn, but not together. They are fantastic actors but have very little chemistry on screen.

Prateek's neighbour is busy making formula for her baby. She has already fed him once. The cap of her thermos flask falls and rolls towards me. I grimace but hand it over. She rinses the lid carefully in her teacup. The baby watches me closely.

A young father walks down from business class, a small baby in his arms. He is crooning 'Chanda Hai Tu' from *Aradhana*. My mother used to sing it to me.

The man seems to be my age. He too must have grown up listening to it. *Why not sing something more recent?* I think, but I cannot blame him. I have not heard a lullaby in a film in years. *Is his wife sleeping?* I wonder. *Is that why he's holding the baby?*

Prateek sleeps beside me, his mouth slightly open, oblivious to his surroundings. I look at him tenderly. He has planned our honeymoon so meticulously: a visit to the Colosseum in Rome, a trip to the Leaning Tower of Pisa, a walk through the ruins of Pompeii and Mount Vesuvius and even a stop in Naples to taste the original Margherita pizza. After that, we will go to Venice for four days, take a gondola ride, and spend time by ourselves. 'Our real honeymoon,' he had told me.

All this planning has taken a toll. No wonder Prateek is tired.

The air hostess walks in, pushing a trolley with our meals. I smile. It has been three hours since she served snacks. I had begun to feel hungry again.

'Veg or non-veg?' she asks briskly.

'Non-veg,' I say.

'Veg,' says Prateek sleepily.

I happily tuck into chicken curry and rice. Prateek opens his tray of palak paneer and rice.

'Yuck,' I say.

'What's so yucky about it?' he demands. He is always a grouch after waking up.

'If I had to eat ghaas-phoos, I should have been a goat,' I say.

Prateek smiles. He likes to see me happy. I am far too serious, according to him.

I look at the woman in the front row. She is so lucky. She hasn't breastfed the baby, nor has she made formula. Even when she goes to the bathroom and hands the baby to her husband, the baby doesn't stir. It's been six hours now. A baby is fed on demand. He should have been fed twice by now. Maybe he really is ill.

When the woman returns, the baby remains under the blanket. One cannot even see his face. *He must be unwell,* I conclude.

The plane hits a pocket of turbulence. The air hostess announces that the use of the lavatory is prohibited and asks passengers to return to their seats. I curse under my breath. I shouldn't have left my visit to the loo so late. I hope the turbulence does not last long.

It subsides soon. The seatbelt sign goes off. Prateek has dozed off again. I get up and walk towards the washroom, casting a curious glance at the couple in the front row. I decide I will ask Prateek to book front-row seats next time, even if it costs more.

After using the washroom, I stop by the galley to get a glass of water. I see the air hostess putting away trays.

She smiles. I say quickly, 'Listen, I am a doctor. The baby in the front row has not stirred at all. I am worried. Please let me know if any help is needed.'

'I am worried myself. I am a young mother,' she replies in a low voice.

'Perhaps you can try to check on the baby,' I suggest.

She smiles reassuringly, but doesn't return to our cabin.

At least I have tried, I think to myself and shrug.

A little later, the pilot announces that the plane has begun its descent. 'Please fasten your seatbelts,' the air hostess instructs.

She tells the man in the front seat to pull up the window shade and to push his seat forward. She asks the woman to fasten her belt.

'My seatbelt is fastened,' the woman mutters.

'I need to see it,' says the air hostess firmly. 'Your blanket is covering the seatbelt.' She removes the blanket. 'Here, let me hold the baby,' she says, reaching down.

The mother tries to snatch the baby back. The air hostess

holds on. Something is wrong. I can see it in her face. I get up, and she quickly hands the baby to me.

The baby is cold. I have seen such babies in the paediatric wards, when we turn to the parents, our faces leaden, and say, 'I am sorry. The baby is no more.'

I look closely at the child—and see a heartbreakingly familiar face. A dimpled chin. A mole.

This is Anmol, the missing baby whose photograph I saw in the newspaper. I lift his shirt and see a gash running down his abdomen. He has been used as a drug mule.

How can someone murder a baby to transport drugs? I feel sick.

How did the woman get past security? Maybe seeing a baby in her arms, the personnel became lax.

The woman lashes out at me. I duck. The flight purser grabs the husband, and the air hostess restrains the woman. Prateek wakes up and looks bewildered.

The plane descends. The police take over. They collect statements. I give them my name and address. I know I will be a witness. The case will drag on.

∽

After what happened to Anmol, I became afraid of having a child. My honeymoon was ruined. I could not enjoy the Colosseum or the Leaning Tower of Pisa. All I could see was Anmol's face.

The case dragged on for ten years. I gave my testimony nine years ago. The judgment was announced just two days before our second honeymoon. The culprits received twenty years' imprisonment—ten already served as undertrials.

According to me, it is not enough. I would have preferred

the death sentence. This was the 'rarest of rare crime', which merits capital punishment.

The pilot's announcement that we are beginning our descent breaks my reverie. I am back in the present.

Prateek looks at me pensively. I know he, too, is reliving the past.

He whispers, 'This time we will celebrate in style. We will revisit all the places we went to during our honeymoon.'

Ten years is a long time. Even Anmol's parents have tried to move on. They now have twins: Arpit and Avantika. Prateek and I have been married for ten years, but we still have no children. I see a flicker of longing in his eyes. He says nothing. He thinks I haven't healed.

He tells me, 'Next year we will go to Switzerland—Geneva, Bern, Interlaken, Zurich. I have already started saving air miles.'

It is time to tell him my secret.

I smile and say, 'I wonder what the cost of an infant ticket is!'

I love the look of wonder on his face.

9

Climb Every Mountain

It is a day like no other.

I am lying in bed with my eyes closed when I am suddenly plagued by an old nightmare—of slipping down a mountainside, clutching at rocks to get a foothold, and then, as my grip loosens, plummeting into the abyss below.

The door opens.

Sujoy is standing there. 'Pa, are you sleeping? Aren't you ready to leave?' he says accusingly.

I get up with a start. 'Of course, I am ready. See, I am fully dressed,' I reply.

'Then let's go,' he says, pulling my hand.

I recall my father-in-law's cryptic summons: 'Meet me at the City Hospital.' I dread the thought of going. I always expect the worst. Sujoy's face is an admixture of hope and apprehension. He does not know what to expect.

As we leave, Sujoy says, 'Pa, tell me about Ma. Tell me about how you met her.'

'You know the story. You have heard it so many times,' I say.

'I never get tired of listening to it,' he responds.

I turn towards him, feeling nostalgic. We are in Kolkata but I am transported back to Sikkim, where I first met her.

It was my first visit to Sikkim, and I fell under its spell almost immediately. The Teesta river, along which the taxi driver drove, stretched endlessly. There was an exhilaration in the mountain air. At night, the inky, star-studded sky was mesmerizing.

On the last day of the retreat, our team visited Nathu La Pass. Reopened only in 2006, it had become the favoured route for the Kailash Mansarovar Yatra.

Just as we were nearing our destination, a girl stopped near our vehicle. 'Lift, please,' she pleaded.

I looked at her and could not stop staring.

'There isn't any place,' I began to say, but she did not hear me.

'Thanks,' she said quickly, squeezing herself into a space in the jeep I did not know existed.

'I am Neha. The jeep I was travelling in broke down.'

I was not sure if that was true or a story she had spun.

We stopped a short distance from the pass. She stepped out and began taking big gulps of air.

'It's altitude sickness,' I said knowledgeably.

'Don't worry. I don't get altitude sickness,' she said, swinging her glorious mane from side to side, her face radiant. 'For me, this air is an elixir—it rejuvenates me. I find mountains exhilarating. I want to climb every mountain.'

A little later, we were at Nathu La Pass. Her eyes crinkled

with joy as she climbed and saw the Indian and Chinese soldiers patrolling the border.

'Wow!' she shouted. 'I am on top of the world!'

She seemed so ephemeral that I was afraid she might suddenly disappear.

That evening, as I came down to the hotel restaurant for dinner, I saw Neha sitting alone at a table. I was glad I had chosen to stay at the Mayfair and not with the rest of the retreat participants.

'How are you here?' I asked.

'I am staying here. I am doing a story about Sikkim. Tomorrow I am going to Char Dham. Why don't you come along?'

'I can't,' I said. 'I am returning to Kolkata tomorrow.'

'It's a weekend, isn't it?' she said, and I decided to cancel my ticket and stay.

I knew I was having the adventure of my life. Was it love? I did not know. I did not believe in love at first sight—but looking at Neha, with her almond eyes and high cheekbones, I was not sure.

'You are only half-alive if you do not do anything with passion. You must live life king-size,' she chuckled.

The next morning, we left for Char Dham. I glanced at Neha—her windswept hair, kohl-lined eyes, dimples flashing every time she laughed, and her complete lack of inhibitions. Char Dham came as a complete surprise. I was enraptured by the 87-foot-high statue of Lord Shiva and the replicas of the Puri, Dwarka, Badrinath and Rameswaram temples.

'Now that you have visited the four dhams, your *moksha* is assured,' Neha laughed when I completed my *darshan*.

'You are mocking me,' I said testily.

'Of course I am, since you have not learnt to laugh at yourself,' she teased. Her husky laughter was the most beautiful sound in the world.

Leaving me behind, she clambered up the steps two at a time until she reached the Shiva statue.

'Mountain goat,' I jeered, panting as I followed.

'I have done a course in mountain climbing,' she retorted. 'I have climbed several small peaks. But I still have my dream mountains—Mount Kilimanjaro, K2, Kanchenjunga, and of course Mount Everest.'

Back in Kolkata, I realized Neha had pervaded my senses. I needed to talk to her, but we had not exchanged numbers. I took a chance and rang up the Mayfair Hotel. She came on the line immediately.

'Are we soulmates?' she asked. 'I was just thinking of you.'

I could imagine her eyes crinkling and her dimples flashing.

'I will come next week and tell you personally,' I threatened. 'Where will you be?'

'Still at the Mayfair. I am visiting the Rumtek Monastery next.'

The next weekend, I took a flight to Bagdogra and drove to Gangtok. We spent a day just walking around the city, breathing the mountain air. The next day, inside the hotel room, we made love. She was satiny soft and silken. As I traced her face with my fingers, I felt waves of tenderness. Somehow it felt so right.

We talked about love and life, our dreams and our future. I told her my dream of getting admission to Harvard Business School was about to come true.

'I will never let anything come in the way of my dream,' I said.

'Neither would I,' she replied.

I smiled. I knew she was someone I would love and cherish for the rest of my life. I decided I would ask her to marry me when I returned from the United States.

I met Neha before I left and told her to wait for me.

In Boston, her presence overwhelmed me. She tiptoed into my dreams. She danced before my eyes. She even appeared in the texts I read in the Harvard library.

I emailed her frequently, telling her how much I missed her. Neha turned out to be a lackadaisical correspondent—chirpy and light-hearted at first, moody and distant later. And then, a few months in, she disappeared. No word, no message, no post.

I tried calling her, emailing, even reaching out on Facebook, but there was no news of her.

I grew bitter. If she had wanted to break up, she could've just said so. Maybe the relationship was only a brief adventure for her. Maybe she had found someone who shared her love of the mountains. That thought hurt like hell.

I did not know how to contact her, so I tried to forget her. I buried myself in a summer internship after first year and returned to India only after completing my MBA.

Back in India, I admitted to myself that Neha was not some distant memory. If I closed my eyes, she appeared instantly. I could hear her laughter in my ears.

There was just one thing to do—I had to find her.

I knew her dream peaks: Kilimanjaro, Kanchenjunga, K2, Everest. I began with Kanchenjunga because Darjeeling was closest.

The hotel I had booked in Darjeeling had a breathtaking view of the Kanchenjunga. I imagined Neha atop the peak.

The next day, I went to the Himalayan Mountaineering

Institute. They would have records of any expeditions she may have participated in.

I had just reached the gate when a little boy came running towards me.

He reminded me of someone. Me. How I looked in my childhood photos.

Then Neha appeared, radiant, her hair swinging.

I gaped. Was she real or a mirage?

She laughed—deep-throated and husky, which filled the air.

'Where did you disappear?' I asked.

She smiled. 'This is my home.'

And the penny dropped. She was the daughter of Major General Kathpalia, the Director of HMI, who had climbed Everest twice. Now I knew where her passion for mountains came from.

'Neha, why did you vanish?' My voice cracked.

She traced her finger across my face. 'I did not want to stand between you and your dreams. I did not want to hold you back because of Sujoy.'

'I deserved to know.'

'You needed to fulfil your dream; you needed to complete your MBA. I did not want to emotionally blackmail you,' she argued.

I noticed the faint lines around her eyes and wondered how she had managed to face it all alone—the pregnancy, the challenges of being a single mother, maintaining her career as a journalist and her love for the mountains. I realized I already knew the answer to that. Neha wanted everything life had to offer and was not willing to give up on any of it.

It must have been hard on her. There must have been nights when she cried herself to sleep. Perhaps she feared I would begin to resent her if I returned for her halfway through my MBA. I now understood why she had disappeared from my life soon after I left for Boston.

'What if I had never found you?' I asked, half-laughing, half-crying, as I looked at the little boy—my son.

'I knew you would find me—if you really wanted to,' she said. 'I am wherever the mountains are.'

I pulled her into my arms. 'Climb every mountain, my love. And when you're back, I will be waiting.'

Life would always be an adventure with Neha. But I would have it no other way. Neha was my anchor, and this time I would not let her go.

After we married, Neha climbed her dream peaks—Kanchenjunga, K2, Kilimanjaro. My heart swelled with pride whenever I saw her pictures after conquering the summits.

Then she undertook the biggest adventure of her life—Mount Everest.

'It an easier to climb than K2. Don't worry, I will be fine,' she said.

I tried to be brave for her and for Sujoy. When her team reached the Everest summit, I heaved a sigh of relief.

I had no idea about the avalanche that hit them on their descent. There was no trace of the team for hours. Rescue missions were sent. Some were injured, some dead.

My father-in-law had not said whether Neha had survived. He only said they were being flown to the City Hospital in Kolkata. He was flying in from Bagdogra.

∽

Sujoy and I reach the hospital. My father-in-law is waiting at the portico. He envelops me in a bear hug and weeps. I have never seen him cry before. He has always been stoic.

I try to be brave and offer a smile, although I realize I should have guessed the truth. Only the dead are brought home; the injured go to Kathmandu.

We walk fast through the hospital. I trail behind, numb.

Then he says, 'We may just be in time to see her—before visiting hours are over.'

I stop.

'Is Neha alive?' I ask, lips trembling.

'Didn't I tell you? She has fractured ribs but she is alive.'

This time I burst into tears.

Sujoy slips his little hand into mine and squeezes.

He has always believed in miracles.

Now I begin to believe too.

10

Revathi

Sunidhi walked into my study, her face tense. I looked up but said nothing. She hesitated, then placed her hand on my shoulder and said, 'Advait, I want to say something.'

I dropped my pen, shut my laptop and turned to give her my undivided attention. Every time she looked at me, I felt as though something momentous had occurred, as though the earth had stood still or the moon had come spinning through the window. But for the past six months, I had shown no reaction.

She looked upset. In fact, as I watched her closely, I realized she looked stricken. Suddenly she blurted, 'Advait, I have a confession to make. I had an affair with my colleague Roshan.'

She said it in a rush, as though she had rehearsed these lines. I stared at her, my head reeling. *People should not confess to such transgressions*, I thought.

They should keep their affairs under wraps, wallow in a

sense of guilt for having cheated on their partners and then bend backwards to please them their entire life as penance—even when the other may not even be aware of the truth. But they should never confess. Not until caught. And yet, Sunidhi had done just that.

I couldn't understand how she could say the words aloud so easily. Words that devastate. Words that slice through in an instant. Why tell me? Why not let me live in ignorance? Why not let life continue as it was—before the accident? Me, making scrambled eggs and toast for breakfast, pouring her a glass of orange juice before she left for work, her coming home, resting her head on my shoulder, munching on microwaved popcorn, watching cricket or a film.

I had never questioned her late hours at work, assuming it was the commute. I had never shown interest in her colleagues or doubted her when she travelled for conferences. Then why confess now? To shed guilt? Or was it out of shame?

I did not react. Earlier, I would have raged. But Sunidhi had been a calming influence. She had taught me patience, equanimity. I had learnt to control my emotions because of her. I processed her words silently, watching my world fall apart in front of my eyes.

I struggled to speak. Finally, I managed a single word. 'Why?'

'Why did it happen? I guess because we were alone after the seminar in Chandigarh. We had a lot to drink and it just happened.'

I shook my head imperceptibly and repeated, 'Why?'

She frowned. 'Why did I tell you? Because you have the right to know the truth.'

I believed we had the perfect marriage. It seemed so ideal

that we remained absorbed in each other even after losing our daughter. I thought couples got married and remained faithful to one another for life, no matter what.

But I was mistaken. I thought Sunidhi was supportive and caring through my depression. I thought I would have recognized any cracks in our marriage. Again, I was wrong.

'Well, what have you decided?' she asked.

I continued to sit on the sofa, unable to react.

'You have nothing to say to me? No accusations, no recriminations, no anger? No reaction at all?' she pressed.

She sounded more angry than guilty or repentant. But I stayed quiet.

She walked to the door, opened it and went out of the house. A little later I heard the sound of a car engine. I assumed she had left me to go to Roshan's house. Under the circumstances, it was the only assumption I could make. I guessed that was the reason she had even confessed. She could have simply said, 'Advait, I am leaving you.' I wondered why she had not.

I sat like a zombie in my armchair. I remembered our seventh anniversary. We did not notice Revathi climbing on to the chair and leaning over the balcony. We did not hear the chair topple over or see her fall. We did not hear her anguished cry as she plunged down, her head smashing against the concrete. We only came to know what had happened when the doorbell rang incessantly.

I had lost my daughter, my only child, and had not even realized it. I had been so absorbed in gazing into Sunidhi's eyes, enraptured by the love I saw in them that I failed Revathi as a father.

I looked at my watch. It was 10 p.m. I went out on to the

balcony to confirm Sunidhi had taken the car, but her vehicle was still parked outside. She must have left on foot. Horrific images flooded my mind: Sunidhi lying on the road, bruised and traumatized; Sunidhi raped; Sunidhi dead. Delhi was not safe for women, especially not at night.

Blood rushed to my head. The inertia of the past six months melted away. I slipped on my shoes, locked the door and rushed down the stairs, unwilling to waste time waiting for the lift. Then I walked outside the gate to look for her.

I found her ten minutes later. She was walking slowly, her head bowed. A man walked a few feet behind her. Maybe he was following her.

I ran up and punched him hard. He staggered and turned to look at me in shock. I recognized him as someone from our apartment complex.

'What is wrong with you? Why did you hit me?' he shouted.

Sunidhi turned. 'Advait, are you all right?' she asked, her voice full of concern.

'Yes,' I said—and then I began to cry. She placed her hand on my shoulder and led me to the bench at the bus stop. We sat in silence for a while. Then she said, 'Advait, I did not.'

She did not have to explain. I understood she had lied about her affair.

'Dr Mohan rang me today,' she said.

I frowned. 'Dr Mohan?'

'Your boss, Dr Chandra Mohan,' she clarified. 'He is worried about you. He said you are depressed and distracted at work. You hardly speak to anyone and usually reply in monosyllables. You just observe, not participate, during meetings. It has been six months since the tragedy… He had hoped you would have recovered by now… He also mentioned that promotions are coming up. He wanted me to coax you back to yourself. You used to be the star performer.'

She paused before continuing. 'I know you have been seeing a psychiatrist, but you are not making much progress. Before Revathi's death, you were different, quick to react. I thought if I confessed to an affair, you would fly into a rage. When you did not react at all, I was so disappointed I had to step out of the house and calm myself.'

'Are you crazy?' I shouted. 'Don't you know what it's like out here? Haven't you read the crime statistics? I have already lost Revathi—I cannot afford to lose you too. You are all I have left in this world!'

My emotions, which had been caged inside me, burst forth. At the mention of Revathi, Sunidhi began to weep. I looked at my wife. She too had lost her daughter, but had tried to hold herself together when she saw I was crumbling and sinking into depression. She had even tried to provoke me into anger through a lie, but had failed.

I would never get over Revathi's death, but at least I still had Sunidhi. As I held her hand, she spoke again. 'Revathi will never come back, but Advait, there are other children in this world who need love and care, Maybe we can find it in ourselves to adopt a child. To share our love again.'

My eyes welled up.

One day, some day, we would learn to be happy again. At least we could try. We owed it to ourselves—and to Revathi.

11

Trust, Borrowed and Broken

Lily stood bleary-eyed on the pavement as she watched the taxi move away.

'Bye Lily!' shouted Memsaab, waving at her through the window.

She waved back diffidently. Once she returned to the flat and locked the door, she let out a whoop of joy. Memsaab would be gone for three days. She had the entire house to herself. For these three days she planned to live the life of a Memsaab!

She pirouetted on the marble floor, switched on the stereo and started dancing to the tune of 'Ghungaroo Toot Gaye'. Tired after dancing, she plonked herself on the bed in the bedroom, swung her legs up and lay down. The mattress was soft yet firm, not like the cotton mattress in the servant's quarter where she lived—it had turned lumpy in less than a year.

Lily picked up the remote and switched on the AC. The

blast of cold air made her shiver, so she unfolded the Jaipuri quilt lying at the foot of the bed and covered herself.

For a moment she felt a pang of guilt for betraying Memsaab's trust. Then she told herself that what Memsaab did not know would not hurt her. When she returned, Lily would once again become the docile domestic help she had always been. Besides, it was Memsaab's own fault for being so trusting.

The cool air began to lull Lily to sleep. She had been up early since Memsaab had taken a morning flight. Perhaps she could doze for a while now. After all, no one was expected to come.

She woke up when the doorbell rang. Her eyes flew to the clock. It had been two hours since she had fallen asleep!

She hurried to the door and flung it open. The newspaper-wallah stood at the doorstep, bill in hand.

She sighed. She was not expecting him. 'Memsaab is not at home. Come back after a week,' she said more curtly than she intended.

He looked surprised, shrugged and left.

Lily returned to the bedroom. It was sheer luck, she thought—Memsaab going away for three days and leaving her in charge of the house, although she had instructed Lily to sleep at night in the servant's quarter.

After a while, Lily began to feel hungry. She usually had just tea and toast for breakfast. But that day, she decided to live Memsaab's life.

Instead of her usual tea, she decided to have green tea, like Memsaab. She poured boiling water into a ceramic mug and dropped in a teabag.

'Ugh!' she exclaimed after the first sip. 'This tea tastes awful. Why doesn't Memsaab have elaichi tea, like Nandan and I do during our afternoons off?'

The thought of Nandan made her smile. Nandan was her boyfriend. Others might call him ordinary, she mused, but she loved everything about him—his fiery eyes, the unruly mop of hair that fell on his forehead, the way he ran his fingers through it, his lips that curled into a secret smile when he thought she was not looking.

He worked as a security guard in the housing complex. But Lily knew he was meant for bigger things.

'This is just the beginning. I intend to go places,' he had told her. She had heard the determination in his voice and believed him.

She decided to call him.

'Memsaab has gone to Shimla for three days and has left me in charge of the house. Why don't you come over?' she asked.

He hesitated. 'I work as a security guard here. If someone finds me missing and complains, I will lose my job,' he said.

He is so cautious. Not impulsive like me, she thought, grimacing. 'What about lunchtime?' she asked, her voice soft.

He seemed to ponder. Perhaps he could sense the disappointment in her voice. 'Okay, I'll come at 1 p.m.,' he said finally.

She smiled as he cut the call.

Lily wondered what to serve Nandan. There were containers of rice, palak paneer, arhar dal and bhindi in the fridge. She decided to cut some green salad and make chapattis. They would eat at the dining table, as if they were the house owners, using the bone china dinner set and silverware.

With two hours to kill before Nandan arrived, Lily decided to have a real bath—not the hurried bucket-and-mug one in the servant's quarter she had every day.

She shampooed her hair and applied body wash, hoping Memsaab would not notice that they had been used in her absence. After drying off with the ultra-soft towel on the handrail—promising herself she would wash it before Memsaab returned—she looked longingly at the bathrobe hanging on the door but resisted the urge.

She got dressed, then sat at the dressing table, gently brushing her hair. She massaged lotion on to her face, dabbed on powder, applied lipstick and added a stroke of kajal. On an impulse, she applied a touch of rouge on her cheeks. She smiled as she saw her reflection in the mirror. She thought she looked like a film star—perhaps Alia Bhatt or Kriti Sanon.

Then she waited for Nandan.

She was not worried he would take advantage of her. He was not that kind of man. They had gone out half a dozen times, but they had only held hands. On occasion, she had seen something in his eyes—longing, perhaps? Or desire? But what could they do? They could only meet for half an hour at a local dhaba, over tea and samosas.

Maybe in the seclusion of Memsaab's home, they would share a kiss. The rest would wait till they married. One of her friends had gotten pregnant before marriage, but Lily had promised herself she would never do anything foolish. She was a good girl.

She shuddered as she thought of that fateful afternoon she fled her home in Ranchi. Her mother had been at work at the garment factory when their neighbour, Ramesh, crept into their tenement. She had been squatting, filling water from the tap, when suddenly his strong arms were around her chest. His whisky-laden breath choked her as he began groping her with one hand.

She jabbed her elbow into his chest and kicked him in the groin. Then, grabbing her purse, she fled before he could recover. She did not stop or look back until she reached the bus stop and boarded the first bus that came by—luckily heading to the railway station.

On impulse, she took a train to New Delhi. She had just enough money for the ticket. She was hungry, and was grateful to a kind family travelling with her, who offered her poori and sabzi. When they arrived at New Delhi Railway Station, the enormity of what she had done hit her. She began to sob.

Memsaab, who had also been on the train, found her crying on a bench. She had asked what was wrong, brought her home and even informed her mother about her whereabouts. Lily shuddered to think what might have happened if she had not escaped—or if Memsaab had not rescued her.

ᔕ

Karuna waited impatiently at Indira Gandhi International Airport. Her flight to Shimla had been delayed. After three hours, she heard the announcement that it had been cancelled.

She could have screamed in frustration. She had got up early, left the house by 7 a.m., arrived two hours before departure, waited another three hours to board the flight due to repeated delays and finally learnt it was cancelled.

She was dismayed. She needed to be in Shimla the next day to inaugurate a workshop on *Gender and Violence*. The topic was close to her heart and aligned with her NGO's mission.

There were no other flights that day.

'I will have to take a taxi,' she sighed, booking an Uber home.

As the taxi sped along, she thought she would heat up the

food in the fridge or just make herself a tomato and cheese sandwich.

As she walked towards her flat, someone called her name. A sub-inspector from the police station stepped forward.

'I'm Ashok Chakravarty, ma'am. I have come for your passport verification.'

Karuna had completely forgotten about it. *Maybe that is why my flight was cancelled*, she thought resignedly.

She had applied for passport renewal just four days ago. She had not realized verification happened so quickly these days. She needed it for her upcoming trip to the US to visit Naitik. It had been a while since she had seen him.

Long-distance marriages did not really work, she thought. She would have to resign from her job. It was a decision she had been avoiding for far too long.

She turned the key in the lock. The door swung open soundlessly.

From the passage, she saw the bedroom door flung wide. Nandan—the boy who guarded the society's houses and cars—stood near the bed, an iron rod in his hand.

'Drop it,' said the sub-inspector behind her, his voice sharp.

Nandan turned in surprise. The rod clattered to the floor. He tried to push past Karuna, but the officer caught him.

Karuna stepped into the bedroom and took in the scene in a single glance.

Lily lay sprawled on the bed, seemingly lifeless, her lipstick smudged. A pillow lay on the floor. *Did Nandan smother her with a pillow?* thought Karuna in alarm.

She was not sure whether Lily was dead. Perhaps Nandan had not been certain either. Maybe that is why he had the iron rod in his hand—to finish the job before leaving with the trinkets he had piled on the table: some silverware, her old iPhone, her camera and her iPad.

Karuna wondered how much it would have fetched him. Not much, she reckoned. *Is human life so cheap?* she wondered.

She felt a wave of pity for Lily. 'I have called for an ambulance and informed the police control room,' said the sub-inspector.

Karuna closed her eyes for a moment, then opened them and reached for Lily's wrist. She thought she felt a slight pulse. She hoped she was right.

She closed her eyes again and began to pray.

12

Childhood Monsters

Sometimes the demons that haunt us in childhood return later in life, when we least expect them.

That evening, when I walked into Sapna's house in Golf Links, I had no premonition of this. All I was looking for was a bit of relaxation. The afternoon had been more acrimonious than I liked—though I knew I was partly to blame.

Instead of taking the conventional stand—that children are innocent and must be treated as such—I had taken the contrarian view: that when children commit adult crimes, they should be treated as adults and punished accordingly. I may have won favour with government officials but among my friends from the NGO world I had stirred deep unease. Some felt betrayed.

But we are all shaped by our memories and circumstances, and during my formative years I had an experience that fuelled this belief. Later, as a lawyer, I had come across many cases where boys in their early teens had raped or murdered. I genuinely did not believe that all they deserved was a brief stay in a juvenile home. I had not minced words while expressing my stance. The juvenile accused in the Nirbhaya case was fresh in my mind.

My sister Sapna's house was close to the India International Centre (IIC) in New Delhi. I strolled down the road to the house, hoping for some respite from the day. My sister's eyes widened in surprise when she saw me.

As soon as I stepped inside, she called for the maid to bring us tea.

'What brings you here, Sameer?' she asked.

'I was attending a seminar at IIC. In fact, I was the keynote speaker,' I said, trying to sound modest.

'What was the seminar about?' she asked absently.

'A debate on whether children under sixteen should be treated as adults when they commit adult crimes.'

'I know your views on that,' she said sombrely.

I knew her mind had immediately flown to the incident that had traumatized us both as children.

It was the summer of 1993. We had flown to London for our summer holidays—an adventure of a lifetime. We could never have afforded it on our own, but Rajnish Mama had sent tickets to Ma, making the trip possible. My father had been uneasy accepting the offer, but seeing our delight he gave in with good grace.

Everything about London delighted us: Tower Bridge, Trafalgar Square, the Thames, Hyde Park, Madame Tussauds, the British Museum. Even the constant drizzle and the dark, dismal sky did not dampen our spirits. It was a welcome contrast to India's enervating summer.

We were there for a month, determined to savour every

moment. About two weeks in, we accompanied our aunt and mother to Southall for grocery shopping.

'We're just picking up a few things. You will get bored,' Ma warned, but we insisted on going.

The mall was bustling. Women pushed trolleys with children in tow—some clinging to arms, some strapped into harnesses, some perched right in the trolleys.

After some time, Sapna and I got bored and started running up and down the aisles while Rekha Mami and Ma finished their shopping. Rekha Mami frowned. She was not used to such unruly behaviour. Perhaps children brought up in the UK were more restrained.

While they lined up at the checkout, Ma told us to go out and play.

We remembered seeing a woman in line behind them, holding the hand of her curly-haired son. A few minutes later, we heard a scream.

We rushed back in and saw the woman who had been standing behind Ma in the queue shouting, 'Where's my son? Has anyone seen my son?'

Panic erupted. Everyone started looking for the little boy. The security guard arrived and began questioning shoppers, but no one had seen the child leave. Neither Mami nor Ma had noticed anything. Neither, for that matter, had we.

We left the mall shortly after.

A few hours later, we got to know from news coverage on TV that the boy had probably been kidnapped. Two days later, the horror emerged: two ten-year-old boys had led him away to the railway tracks, pelted him with stones and killed him.

'Monsters,' Sapna seethed. I agreed.

Ma said, 'What is even worse is that they will get away

with it as they are ten-year-olds. They will probably just be sent to a detention home for three years.'

But she was wrong. She was citing the law that prevailed in India, not in the UK.

The court found the boys guilty of murder and sentenced them to prison. The judgment stated that a child who commits an adult crime should receive a proportionate punishment.

Both Sapna and I were glad. We believed the boys deserved to rot in jail. We wished we had been more alert—maybe we could have seen them leading the boy away.

The incident scarred us for life. It taught us not to trust blindly. For me, the care and protection of children became a personal crusade. I also understood that the belief that all children are innocent is not universally true. That experience shaped me.

'God, I am exhausted,' I declared, stretching out in the armchair.

'Do you want pakoras?' Sapna asked.

I was glad she did. I'd skipped the post-seminar tea and was beginning to feel famished. Besides being an ace lawyer, Sapna was a wizard at cooking.

She disappeared into the kitchen.

I heard jars opening, pans clanging. Fifteen minutes later, she emerged with a plate of pakoras. There was a fluidity to her movements as she placed four of them on my plate—she reminded me of a dancer, which made sense. She had trained in Kathak but gave it up after marriage.

'Marriage, career and dance?' she'd laughed when I asked her why she stopped. 'Sameer, I am not Wonder Woman.'

'Where is Aman?' I asked as I began eating. 'I have brought him a present. Hope he likes it.'

'You spoil him too much,' she said. 'You really shouldn't bring him a toy every time you visit us.'

Suddenly the door burst open. Madhav, Sapna's nephew, stood in the doorway, panting as though he had run a mile.

'Chachi,' he gasped, breathless. 'I found Aman's bicycle on the ground near the park—but he is nowhere to be seen.'

Sapna took off, unmindful of the fact that she was leaving the front door wide open. I followed her, but not before hollering to the maid to shut it. Unlike Sapna, I am always cautious.

Sapna and Madhav raced ahead. The park was not far, and I soon caught up with them. Aman's bicycle lay sprawled on the pavement. Nearby, a large stone was stained with blood.

Sapna swooned at the sight and collapsed on to the pavement. I recalled her phobia of blood. Even the smallest cut had always made her feel faint. I carefully lifted her and laid her on a bench inside the park. She began to stir almost immediately.

'Oh my God. Where is Aman? How badly is he hurt? Why didn't he come home if he was injured? Did someone hit him deliberately?' Her volley of questions left Madhav speechless.

'Chachi, I do not know,' he said quietly. 'I just saw Aman's bicycle and ran home to tell you.'

Sapna broke down, sobbing—a far cry from the poised woman of a few minutes ago.

'Let's go home and decide what to do,' I said gently.

But she shook her head. She knew time was of the essence. 'If anyone took Aman on foot, they could not have gone far,' she said urgently. 'Should we call the police?'

'Let's search first,' I suggested tentatively.

She agreed. We decided to spread out and look in different directions.

Just then, Kanishka, Madhav's classmate who had been playing nearby, came running up. 'I saw Aman playing with two other boys,' he said. 'One was tall, the other had curly hair.'

'Do you know who they are?' I asked.

'They're from our school. We all take the same bus,' he said, and started crossing the road. 'I know where one of them lives,' he added, walking towards Pandara Road.

We followed him to a mustard-coloured house. He unlatched the gate, walked up to the front door and rang the bell.

A lady opened it almost at once. 'Yes?' she said, polite curiosity in her eyes.

'Is your son at home?' Sapna's voice was sharp, almost accusatory. I realized how little it takes to transform a woman into a lioness.

'Why are you asking?' the woman replied, now clearly concerned about her son's safety.

'Where is he?' Sapna asked, her voice mildly hysterical.

'Anand has gone to the park with a friend,' the woman replied, taking in Sapna's expression.

'My son's bicycle is lying on the pavement with a blood-stained stone next to it,' Sapna said, her voice shaking. 'Someone saw Aman with your son and another boy. I want to know where they have taken him.'

I could see what was tormenting her: the image of two older boys leading seven-year-old Aman away, pelting him with stones. We were no longer in 2019. We were back in 1993. Some nightmares never fade. This was one of them.

'If anything happens to my son, I will not spare yours,' Sapna threatened.

The woman's face softened and she gently said, 'Come with me. I think I know where they've gone.'

She locked the door and began walking briskly down the road. A few minutes later, she turned into a cream-coloured building.

Is this it? I wondered. A deserted place? My stomach tightened.

As she stepped inside, a curly-haired boy rushed towards her. Grabbing her arm, he said breathlessly, 'Mummy, thank God you are here. A boy from school—Aman—was riding his bicycle when he fell and hit his head. He started bleeding a lot and got scared to go home, so we brought him to the dispensary.'

'You did the right thing,' she said, patting his back. He beamed at her, proud.

We followed them quickly into the dispensary. Aman was seated quietly while a nurse finished dressing a head wound.

'We are taping the wound. Thankfully it is not deep and will not need stitches,' the doctor informed us. 'He's also been given an anti-tetanus injection.'

Aman looked like an injured warrior. His lips were trembling, but he was trying not to cry. Sapna rushed to him, then turned to the curly-haired boy and hugged him tightly, her tears flowing freely. She didn't need to say anything. Her embrace said it all.

The boy's mother smiled. 'I'm Dr Raksha Purohit. I work here,' she said in a kind voice. 'I have taught my son to come straight to the dispensary if someone gets hurt, and to make sure they get a tetanus shot.'

Sapna, still weeping, nodded her thanks.

That day, both Sapna and I decided to lay our childhood ghosts to rest. Not every young boy is a monster. Most are like Anand. We needed to remember that.

13

The Boy Next Door

Did you ever sit by the window and watch the world go by? No, you did not. You were too busy being a part of that world. You zipped along on your scooter or your car, racing down tarred roads, the wind blowing in your face. At times, when there was a downpour, you skipped along potholed streets, the rain pelting down and drenching you to the skin. You shivered slightly, suddenly self-conscious at how your cream blouse clung to your body, revealing far more than it concealed.

You never skulked behind a window, as I did—deluged by waves of self-pity, choked with anger, filled with impotent rage against everyone. Particularly Gaurav.

If only he had not coaxed me to accompany him to the Book Fair at Pragati Maidan. If only he had not mesmerized me with his words, painting with deft strokes the magical world of letters. If only he had not mentioned Murakami, Alice Munro and Gabriel García Márquez in one breath. If only he had not insisted I needed a break from studying.

Then my world would not have come crashing down.

I clench my fists to hold back the tears. I do not want them to fall. I want to simmer in rage, fume in silence and rail against the world. Against fate. Against him.

A motorbike sputters in the distance, and then the engine cuts. Gaurav's brown head bobs up and down past my window. He looks like a puppet on a string. His new leather shoes crackle on the stairs. I hope they pinch. His shadow precedes him. Then he is at the doorway, standing before me. All six feet two inches of him.

'Vanita.' The word dies in his throat.

I have never seen him fumble with words before. They always glided from his lips, a cascade of brilliance and ease. Today he is almost tongue-tied. But I know what he wants to say. I can anticipate it.

I'm sorry.

Sorry. That umbrella phrase that tries to cover everything: I am sorry I missed your birthday. I am sorry I could not make it to your convocation. I am sorry about your leg.

But instead, Gaurav says, 'Vanita, I came to say goodbye.'

I'm stunned. This is not what I expected. I expected sorrow. Profuse apologies. Not this abrupt declaration of departure. But his voice is heavy with guilt. Or maybe it is just my imagination.

I look away. I say nothing. I have not spoken to Gaurav since I returned from the hospital. I did not speak to him while I was there either. I looked away every time he stood at my bedside.

I do so again.

His shoulders slump. He turns and walks away. His steps

echo down the stairs, slow and leaden. I see him sit astride his motorbike.

Suddenly, I'm flooded with yearning.

Look up, I plead silently. *Look up just once.*

That would tell me he cares. That would be enough.

But he doesn't. He sits stiffly on his motorbike. Then he rides away.

He is gone. For six months. Or a year. Or forever. Who knows.

I kick my leg viciously against the bed.

Correction. The stump.

I kick the stump against the bed. The impact jolts through me and I begin to whimper, which turns into a moan, then a cry. I look at what's left of me—this abhorrent, repellent stump. Once it was a long, graceful leg, tapering into a beautiful foot with elegant arches. My foot. The one that wore the silver anklets Gaurav gave me for my birthday.

I see my dream of becoming a classical dancer—gone. My dream of being a globetrotter—evaporated. People with prosthetic legs aren't expected to go around the world. Their dreams shrink. As does their world.

I look at the prosthetic limb lying on the table beside my bed. I hate it. It's not me. It's alien. It is merely an appendage.

If only we had not gone to the Book Fair.

If only the motorbike had not been going so fast.

If only we had not hit that car.

If only Gaurav had not been flung aside and lost consciousness.

If only my leg had not been pinned under the motorbike for so long.

I have a gift for repetition. My litany of regrets never changes.

'Gaurav has gone,' says Ma.

She makes it sound like a death sentence.

'I will not miss him,' I mutter. Muttering comes easily these days. I mutter expletives in anger all the time.

'Let him go. He has his own life to live,' I say indifferently.

It's a lie.

I feel hollow. There's pain in the pit of my stomach. Like a boxer who has taken a violent punch. His eyes haunt me. So does his voice. I love its cadence. It reminds me of a murmuring brook—the one Tennyson wrote about, the one that goes on forever.

His laughter haunts me too. Everything about him does.

I want to push away the lock of hair that falls on his forehead, the one that makes him screw up his eyes. I want to feel the satin of his skin against mine. I want to hold him tight, hear the wind whisper secrets into his ears as he rides me around on his motorbike. I want to wake up in his arms.

I want this to be a dream. And to laugh aloud when I wake up.

But I touch the stump. It is a rude reminder that my leg is gone. This is my living nightmare.

A young, happy girl has been shorn of her dreams, her future, her joy.

And I blame Gaurav. Without my leg I have no future. I have blamed him for months. I have not forgiven him. I don't know if I ever will.

He is gone, but I know he will keep in touch. I am sure he will write to me. He always does when he goes to Bangalore. I used to look forward to his emails. They were cheerful and amusing and they tickled my funny bone. He has a way with words.

But this time there is only silence. I sense an emptiness I had never felt before. All the clichés I have read in mushy romantic books are true, I realize.

I love him. I love him with every fibre of my being. I would walk to the ends of the earth for him. I would go down on bended knee. I am passionately, madly in love with him.

He is my rock. My anchor. My comfort zone. My mentor. My confidant. My partner in crime.

My cheeks are wet.

Maybe absence really does make the heart grow fonder. And distance too. Another cliché I used to mock.

We've known each other since childhood, despite the three years between us. He taught me to climb trees, then to slither down them. He cleaned my grazed knees with antiseptic and bandaged them. He showed me how to eat raw mangoes with rock salt. He placed a ladybird in my palm and laughed when he heard me squeal with horror.

He taught me the Archimedes principle. The Pythagoras theorem. The causes and consequences of the two World Wars. The meaning of sovereignty. He made me read *Love in the Time of Cholera*.

He taught me how to ride a bicycle. Then a motorbike.

He was always there.

I realized I loved him too late. That day on the bike. When his arms came around me from behind and held me tight.

I thought his embrace would crush me. My heart pounded so loud I feared he would hear it.

That moment was magical.

For me, the motorbike became a flying carpet.

I closed my eyes and wished the ride would never end.

And that's when I lost control of the bike.

It skidded, hit a car, flew into the air, flung Gaurav far away and came crashing down on me, pinioning my leg beneath it.

I felt his hand on my brow as I hovered between consciousness and delirium. He had a healing touch. His hand held mine tight when the doctor broke the news to my mother—that my leg would have to be amputated. But once the operation was over and I regained consciousness, I withdrew from him.

While I was in the hospital, Gaurav stood outside my door every day, his eyes tortured and his face etched with guilt. Once I returned home, he came to the house daily, despite my stony silence and my mother's anguished tears.

He is the man I yearn for now—insanely, achingly. I want him to wrap his arms around me. I want his breath on my face, his lips on mine, his tongue tracing the deep crevices of my mouth. I want his skin against mine, his stubble grazing my cheek, his cologne enveloping me. I want him. Oh God, I want him.

But now there is no chance. Because I am just an amputee. A girl with a stump for a leg. A third-year student of English Honours in Delhi. While he is an engineer from IIT Delhi, now studying at IIM Bangalore for his Postgraduate Diploma in Management.

∽

It is Diwali today and Ma wants me to come out and celebrate.

'Celebrate?' She cannot miss the look of disdain on my face. 'What is there to celebrate?'

'You could call your friends,' she suggests, tentatively.

'I have no friends,' I snap.

I stopped going to college. I could not bear the pitying glances. I would rather wallow in self-pity. Alone.

Although she pleads, I refuse to step out of my room, which has been my haven for months.

'Just how long will this go on?'

I spin around. The voice I would die for echoes in the room. Gaurav stands in the doorway, a big box of sweets in his hands.

'Happy Diwali,' he says.

'What is so happy about Diwali?' I mutter, turning and walking into my room. I shut the door behind me.

I have shut him out. And with him, any chance of happiness.

If I had not lost my leg. If only.

I wait to hear the familiar roar of his motorbike as it pulls out of the portico. But the silence drags. Deafening.

Then my mother's voice breaks it.

'Why do you feel so guilty? It was an accident, after all.'

'I only wish I'd been driving that day,' Gaurav replies. 'If only I had not given in to her demand to ride the motorbike. If only I had put my foot down. But she could always twist me around her little finger.'

I can almost see my mother's eyes widening in horror.

'What are you saying?' she gasps, probably clutching the table for support.

'Yes Ma,' I say, opening the door. 'I was driving the motorbike that day. Not Gaurav.'

'Then why have you been punishing him, when the accident was not his fault?' she demands.

'In a way, it was,' he says quietly. 'If I had not let her drive, if I had insisted, maybe the accident would not have happened.'

'If I had not realized just then that I was in love with him—if I had not closed my eyes—maybe the accident would not have happened either,' I mutter to myself.

Either way, I blame him.

I retreat to my room and slam the door shut.

'Why did you come here every day?' I hear Ma ask, still stunned.

'You know why,' he says.

'I thought you would change your mind after the accident.'

'How can you think that of me? How can you say something like that?' His voice is harsh now. 'I came here every day hoping she would soften—just enough to stop hating me. So I could finally tell her how much I love her.'

I open the door again. They both look at me.

'Gaurav, you don't need to pity me,' I say. 'I can manage. I can walk. See, there is hardly a limp.' I smile satirically and turn back to my room.

'So you don't love me, Vanita? And never will?' he asks.

'Are you blind, Vanita?' Ma says. 'Can't you see the love in his eyes?'

I walk unsteadily into my room and shut the door again.

This time, I hear him walk away. Suddenly I am afraid that this may be the last time.

Why am I angry at him? For letting me drive? For falling in love with him one minute, only to have everything destroyed the next?

Whatever the reason, it has dissipated.

I cannot let him leave. Not again.

I slip on my prosthetic leg and rush down the stairs, unmindful of whether I might trip. My breath comes fast, my heart pounding. At the last step, I see him, just about to kick-start his bike.

'Will you take me for a ride?' I ask.

He turns, startled. 'Are you sure?' he says.

It's the same bike I once hated. The same bike that changed everything.

I nod. 'I want to overcome my fears. I want to feel the wind whisper in my ears. I want it to ruffle your hair. I want my arms around you again. I want the scent of tangerines and grapefruit in your aftershave. I want the satiny feel of your skin on mine. I want raindrops on my face. I want your lips on mine. I want to exult in being alive.'

I have never said anything like this to him before.

He opens his arms in welcome. I let him hold me, just for a moment. But it is enough. I exult in his touch. I hope the euphoria will last forever.

I climb on to the motorbike and hold him tight.

And I know—he will never let me go.

14

The Sound of Silence

Everyone has a favourite song. One that gives wings to their dreams, transports them into another world and touches their soul. I too have a song, though it is dark and melancholic—'The Sound of Silence'. It resonates with me. It haunts me. I found the CD on Papa's study table and played it once. I have never stopped playing it since. The lyrics of Simon and Garfunkel's song strike a chord within me. For silence speaks to me. I am locked in an eternal world of silence.

No, I am not deaf; I can hear everything. But I cannot make sounds that people can hear.

Doctors have a name for people like me. Autistic. I am different from others. I have always been different. I am non-verbal. I am trapped in a world of my own—a world that belongs only to me. I hate intruders. Yet everyone encroaches on my space. The world resonates with sound, while I detest it. I abhor noise. I loathe the cacophony. It's why I hate festivals. Especially Diwali.

I hate it when crackers burst. I hate the sparklers that shimmer and sizzle, the flowerpots that zoom into the sky and then litter the ground with ashes, the bombs and the patakas that explode in a deafening roar.

'Stop!' I want to scream. 'Stop all that noise.'

But all I can get out of my throat is a guttural '*Aaa…argh… aah…*' Meaningless jumbles. That, and the throaty laughter Papa calls 'a mad, maddening laugh'.

Every year on Diwali, once the fireworks begin, I hide under the dark, cavernous double bed in my room. It has dusty steel trunks wedged underneath it. One year I forgot to crawl out and, feeling hungry, forsaken and lonely, I slept under the bed.

Ma and Papa went berserk looking for me. They spent a sleepless night sitting in the drawing room, their faces drawn and their eyes bleary from searching, until I wiggled out from under the bed—still cowering in fear.

'You cannot do that, Rahul, you understand? No more hiding under the bed!' Ma shouted.

Suddenly my haven was taken from me.

The next Diwali, I ran away to the neighbourhood park and hid under a bench near the gate. People celebrate Diwali in their homes, not in the park. I thought I was safe. But darkness fell. All the houses looked the same. And I cannot speak, so I could not tell anyone where I lived.

I sat under the bench and cowered.

Later, a woman came and sat down above me and began sobbing. Though I could not see her, I could smell the turmeric on her saree, the rajnigandha in her hair and the sandalwood on her hands.

Ma, I thought, the word stuck in my throat.

I tugged at her saree. She screamed in fear, then froze as I crawled out from under the bench and stood before her. She hugged me hard and held me tight, as though she would rather die than let me go.

I once heard Ma talking about me to her younger sister, Sneha Mausi.

'I knew there was something wrong with him soon after he was born,' she said. 'He didn't make eye contact and turned away every time I held him.'

It took my parents three years to get me diagnosed. They took me to an institute in Bangalore to find out why I did not speak. They were afraid I was deaf. I underwent many tests. The doctors told them my hearing was fine, but that I was autistic.

'What do you mean, autistic?' Papa had asked. I could see his jaw drop. There is little he does not know—or thinks he does not.

I think Mummy had suspected it all along.

The tears came with the realization that their perfect little world was not so perfect after all. It had been rocked. No, it had crashed. Their priorities had to be reset because they had a differently abled child.

Mummy and Papa became two combatants on opposite sides of a battlefield. They hurled barbs with deadly precision. The blame game unfolded at regular intervals.

'They say autism is genetic. It runs in families,' said Papa.

'There is no autistic person in my family,' Ma snapped.

'But your niece is dyslexic,' Papa countered triumphantly—as though dyslexia and autism are the same, just because the words sound similar.

There is nothing Papa likes about me—neither my ungainly gait, nor my habit of shaking my head from side to side nor my tendency to burst into a song any time, anywhere.

I stick out like a sore thumb. And he cannot bear the stares—curious, censorious or pitying—that come his way because of me. He is a Hiranandani and his family does not brook failure.

And I am his failure.

Aamir Khan once made *Taare Zameen Par* about dyslexic children. I wish he had made one about autistic kids too. But on second thoughts, why should he? I do not want to educate people about autism. Besides, films have been made about children on the spectrum. I saw *My Name Is Khan*. Shah Rukh Khan played a man with Asperger's syndrome.

Papa hates taking me to the Officers' Club. He knows I'll start tapping my feet if the waiter delays our order or burst into my strange 'song'. Of course, my song is just *aaaah*. He calls it cacophony. He cannot peek inside my mind and hear the melody vibrating within.

But I cannot blame Papa. He is like everyone else. They see me as a freak. I'm slowly learning to live with it, although it is difficult.

The other day Papa's cousin and his family came over. As they entered the drawing room, their little daughter saw me shaking my head to music. She screamed and ran out.

'Go to your room, Rahul,' Papa said, his voice low but firm.

I stared at him mutinously.

This is my home, I wanted to say. *I cannot be shunted from my own drawing room. If she doesn't like me, she can stay home. Who wants that short, fair, whey-faced, stupid, moronic girl in my house? Not me.*

But I went inside meekly. Because I cannot speak.

Travelling is traumatic too. When I was younger, Ma would

take me through security with her. But now that I am older, I must manage on my own. Once, at the airport, a duty manager approached Ma.

'Is he likely to create a nuisance?' he asked.

Ma bristled like a porcupine. 'Are all those children at the airport—running around, almost tripping elderly people—not a nuisance?' she retorted. 'Just because my son is shaking his head while listening to music, do you think he's going to cause trouble? Do you not know how to treat differently abled people?'

My education too was a nightmare. I could not go to a regular school, and there were very few special schools where we lived. But Ma persevered and found one for children with special needs—children with cerebral palsy, Down syndrome and the like.

But I was different from the others. While they played, I banged my head against the wall. I wanted to be left alone. I did not want to be part of a crowd. When I bit the hand of the ayah who tried to stop me, Ma knew it was time to withdraw me from school.

She said she had the courage to do so because she suspected I had a high IQ. Ma exaggerates, of course, but she always marvelled at the fact that while she got flummoxed in parking lots full of white cars, I would run to ours like a homing pigeon. And when I took a 500-piece jigsaw puzzle from her room and completed it in a day, she had tears in her eyes.

'I couldn't have done it. I couldn't have done it,' she repeated, as though I had just won the world chess championship or something.

She took me for an IQ test and returned home triumphant. 'He's a high-functioning autistic. He has an IQ of 140. He could gain entry to the Mensa club, meant exclusively for people with high IQ,' she told Papa.

'So what if he is Einstein incarnate? Will he invent something like the theory of relativity? Will he ever go to school?' Papa had shouted.

Ma took up the challenge and decided to homeschool me. She knew I could not speak or respond verbally, but I could hear. She wrote letters of the alphabet on a blackboard and I copied them. She taught me maths the same way. It was an uphill task. I had a very limited attention span. My mind wandered within minutes. Sometimes I wanted to be left alone with my iPad or iPod. Often, I found the lessons boring.

But Ma persisted and slowly her painstaking effort bore fruit. One day I realized I could read the newspaper headlines and even understand them. Although Papa still shared an uneasy relationship with me, his study became my favourite place. I began to devour storybooks and comics.

It was then that Ma introduced me to the magic of cards. She taught me to convey my emotions through them. Happy. Sad. Hungry. Angry. Afraid. She made a stack with illustrations.

'Carry them with you and show a card to convey your feelings,' she said.

Now, if I woke up crying in the middle of the night, I could show her whether I was hungry, scared or in pain.

I still have no friends. But I do not need friends. I am happy in my own world, where I am left undisturbed.

'You must learn to socialize,' Ma told me.

'Mission impossible,' I wrote on a piece of paper and showed her. She laughed.

But life is not simple. It is complicated. As one grows

up, one needs to prepare for the transition from childhood to adolescence. No one prepared me for it. Perhaps Ma and Papa thought I was still a child. I learnt it the hard way.

We were flying from Delhi to Mumbai and Ma was sure she had packed everything—my iPad, iPhone, Kindle. But she had not prepared herself for the unexpected. At the airport, while waiting for our flight, I saw a girl near the bookstall. She was beautiful, or at least I thought so. She looked a little lost and bewildered—like me. My head began to pound. I felt something strange stir inside me. I came behind her and held her tightly. I had seen Papa do it to Ma, and the gardener do it to our maid.

I did not know it was wrong.

She screamed—but like me, her voice made a choking, gurgling sound. Then her father caught me by the collar. Before Ma and Papa realized what had happened, he dragged me to the security staff and said, 'Arrest him.'

Papa rushed forward. 'What happened?' he asked.

'Your son molested my daughter. I will send him to jail,' the man shouted.

'My son is mentally challenged,' Papa said quickly, fumbling in his pocket for the doctor's certificate that attested I was autistic. Ma looked as if she wanted to rebut his statement but then she saw the man's stern face and decided that this was not the time to brag about my IQ.

'Keep your son in harness. He's not safe to be let loose,' the man spat.

Papa's face turned crimson. I could tell he wished he could disown me.

Ma hissed under her breath, '*Barfi* was a film, Rahul. This is real life. Stop acting as if you have met the love of your life.'

But if Barfi, who was deaf, could marry an autistic girl and live happily ever after, why couldn't I? Why did Papa always worry about what would happen to me after he and Ma were gone? Were happy endings meant only for fictional characters?

I hadn't planned to—but almost instinctively, I began to sketch her face in my notebook. I was surprised to discover that I was a good artist. I had captured a fair likeness. Then I sketched myself. I decided I was not the villain her father had made me out to be. I was a hero. And I needed to put it into words—to overcome the humiliation I had felt at the airport.

In the story I began writing, the protagonist was not just a hero. He was a superhero. Like Superman. But with one difference—he couldn't speak. He was autistic. But he had powers. He appeared wherever he was needed. He helped people.

I wrote by hand in a large notebook and kept it locked away. I have no idea how Ma discovered it. But one day, she did. She read what I'd written—whatever there was of it.

'It's a graphic novel,' Ma said excitedly. 'Your illustrations are excellent. You must sit down and complete it.'

For her, this became a new project. I could already see her formulating strategies for how to market the book. Ma knew she had a bestseller on her hands—not because the book was brilliant (it wasn't) but because a non-verbal, autistic teenager had written a graphic novel. Perhaps for the first time ever, at least in India.

And that is how I find myself standing on the stage at the India International Centre in New Delhi—a little intimidated, a little shy, very nervous—clutching my about-to-be-released book in my hand, a book I cannot speak about. But I have my PowerPoint presentation. It will say all I need to say.

And Ma will be my voice.

My story will say that autistic boys can be heroes too. They can fly high.

Provided they too have a hero by their side.

In my case, my ma.

15

The Wait

There is nothing I detest more than the grandfather clock that hangs in our drawing room. It clangs with monotonous regularity every hour, when all I long for is silence. I glare at the walnut frame, the yellowed dial, the brass pendulum. How I would love to throw it out. But I cannot. Not any more. Ronit had bought the clock, and now that he has gone, every relic has assumed the status of an heirloom. Ronit's photo smiles at me sardonically just as the clock begins clanging.

I eye it warily. Twelve o'clock. Amit must have begun his medical entrance examination. So much hinges on that exam. His future and mine; his dream of becoming a doctor—a neurosurgeon. Medical entrance tests are notoriously tough in India, a country with 1.3 billion people but very limited seats. This morning, I sent him off with a bowl of curd and a mithai—our traditional way of wishing good luck.

My stomach growls. I'm hungry. I have not eaten breakfast. I yearn for toast with marmalade or a slice of cheese and a cup of coffee. But I must fast today. Not a morsel till Amit returns.

'Trying to bribe the gods?' Amit had laughed when he learnt I was fasting. But that is how I am—a little traditional, a tad conservative and a complete home bird.

I look up at the wall. Ronit is still smiling that same sardonic smile.

'Laugh. Mock me. Go on,' I say aloud.

I talk to Ronit every day. It is my way of keeping him alive. It is also how I ensure I continue to grieve. I fear that one day I may stop. The marigold garland around his photograph has withered. I need to go to the market and buy a fresh one.

It's been a year since Ronit left us. Amit once suggested I switch to something more permanent. A sandalwood garland, perhaps. But I like marigold best. And going to the market gives me something to do.

The phone rings, startling me. Not my mobile—the landline. It cannot be Amit. It is too soon. I pick it up with trepidation. Few people call me. Even fewer have this number. Who can it be?

The voice on the phone sounds unsteady. 'Vinita. Ravish here. There has been an accident, I am coming to pick you up.'

Ravish Bajaj.

I would have known it was him by the voice even without the name. He is Ronit's friend, and was once my classmate in college. Now I know him as Tanya's father.

Accident. When? Where? How? How is Amit?

I forget to ask all that. I sit on the edge of the bed and weep. I do not know why I am crying. I do not know the magnitude of what's happened.

I dry my eyes. *Ravish is coming to pick me up*, I remind myself. I glance at my crumpled, turmeric-stained saree, which faintly reeks of mustard oil. Should I change? No. It will have to do. I am not going to a celebration. I run a comb through my hair and tie it into a bun.

The doorbell rings. The knot in my stomach tightens. I open the door. Ravish hugs me briefly. I widen my eyes in surprise. The physical proximity unsettles me, though I've known him for years. Does he think he can take liberties now that Ronit is gone? Why am I thinking this? He looks apologetic.

'Amit? Is he...?' I ask quickly.

'He is alive,' Ravish says shortly.

Relief floods me. That's all that matters—for now.

I know Ravish does not mean to be brusque. We all collapse differently under pressure.

He drives fast. Too fast. He jumps red lights, breaks speed limits. As if he has a death wish.

'Don't drive so fast—do you want us to have an accident?' I am about to snap. Then I remember. There has been an accident. That is why we are rushing to the hospital.

We reach the Safdarjung flyover.

'Here is where it happened,' he says. 'The driver hit the speed breaker. The Innova flew into the air, then overturned. Out of the seven children travelling in the car, three died and four are seriously injured. They are at AIIMS.'

Seven bright minds. Just eighteen years old. Three already gone.

'Tanya?' I ask. I realize I should have asked about her earlier.

'Tanya didn't make it,' he says quietly.

I am stunned. Why didn't he tell me sooner?

No wonder he is driving like someone demented. Like me, Ravish had no one in the world except Tanya. His wife Anita left years ago for another man. He was devastated.

I should have asked about Tanya before. I was so wrapped up in my own world I didn't see that his had just shattered.

I do not know what to do now. I've always been awkward with people. A loner. Situations like this scare me.

I raise my hand and rest it gently on his arm. There. It wasn't so difficult after all.

Ravish is like a child now, a child I'm trying to comfort.

'She was all I had,' he says at last, his voice breaking.

I feel his pain. But there's nothing I can do about it.

Thank goodness I still have Amit, I tell myself.

He parks in the hospital lot. I stand at the entrance, lips moving silently in prayer. AIIMS is a premier medical institute. Amit will receive the best care.

I follow Ravish towards the reception, the spur on my foot forgotten.

'I am Amit Sinha's mother—the accident case,' I say at the desk. 'Where is he?'

The receptionist stares blankly. The name rings no bells. I convince myself that it is a good sign.

Someone in the corridor takes charge, leads me to the lift and presses five. We stop at the Neurosurgery ICU. I wince at the irony. Amit dreams of becoming a neurosurgeon. Maybe one day he still will.

The man at the counter hands me a mask and asks me to wear shoe covers. I do so, my hands trembling. I scrub with hand sanitizer. As I walk along the corridor, I hear not a sound. There seems to be a conspiracy of silence.

At last I reach Amit's cubicle. As I push the door open, I

see him—entangled in tubes. He is hooked to a monitor. A ventilator, I realize.

The doctor walks in just after me. He looks sombre. Do all doctors wear that look? Is it because they are so often surrounded by grief?

Amit lies still, almost serene. I hear him breathe. Thank God. He's alive. Tears spill down my face.

'Is he sleeping?' I whisper.

The doctor does not hear me.

'How serious is it?' I ask louder.

He looks at me for a long time, as if weighing something. Then he looks away.

'Amit is in a coma,' he says quietly. 'He has suffered severe brain injuries. His condition is critical.'

'But he will recover, won't he?' I persist.

The doctor says nothing. But I can still hear Amit breathing. I do what I am best at—I pray.

A nurse enters and gestures that it is time for me to leave.

I walk out of the ICU and into the corridor, face mask and shoe covers discarded. The smell of phenyl on the tiled floor is not unpleasant. But it is a grim reminder that in a hospital nearly all patients are waging silent battles against death. No wonder people dread hospitals. No wonder so many ignore symptoms until it is too late.

I want to stay overnight in the waiting room, if the doctors permit. I want to stay near Amit, just in case he wakes up and asks for me.I take the lift to the ground floor. Ravish is waiting outside.

I realize he too has a long wait ahead. It's a police case now. Formalities must be followed before Tanya's body is released. My heart aches for him. I cannot imagine losing a child.

As I walk towards him I see a woman approach. She begins speaking to him softly, earnestly. Her voice is low but urgent. *The NGO type*, I think almost irritably.

I'm right. She belongs to an NGO and is asking him to donate Tanya's eyes.

How insensitive, I think indignantly. *Can't they leave him in peace?*

But Ravish listens, his face unreadable. I expect him to say no. Instead, he nods. She hands him some forms. 'There are other organs you can donate,' she says gently, 'while there's still time.'

Then she turns to me. 'Are you Amit's mother?' she asks. It is more a statement than a question. She has done her homework well.

I nod.

'What about you?' she asks.

'What about me?' I repeat, puzzled.

'Will you also donate?'

'What do you mean?' I snarl. 'My son is alive.'

She pauses, caught off guard. 'I'm sorry,' she says quickly, 'I was told he was brain dead.'

I stare at her, horrified.

She must be mistaken. I want to shake her by the shoulders for spreading such a rumour. But then I recall the doctor's words: 'Coma...severe brain injuries'. I remember the way he had looked away, his silence louder than anything he could have said.

I look at Ravish. He doesn't meet my gaze. He looks at the floor.

Brain dead. Amit was not breathing on his own. The ventilator was keeping him alive. It was giving me the illusion of life. The doctor had been preparing me, slowly, gently, waiting for the right time.

Or maybe it is not true. Maybe Amit will open his eyes. Maybe all of this is a nightmare from which I will wake up. Doctors are not God. Even they make mistakes.

How can I give them permission to turn off the ventilator?

My mind is in a whirl. But one fact registers finally—my son is gone.

I would have collapsed if not for Ravish. He puts his arm around me and I no longer squirm under his touch. We are partners in grief.

I want to howl. To scream. To rail against the unfairness of it all. I lost Ronit barely a year ago. And now Amit—the reason I woke each morning—is gone.

Ravish takes me to the canteen. I sit numbly while he brings two cups of coffee and two club sandwiches. The smell of food nauseates me. I want to throw up. But my stomach is empty. No wonder I'm light-headed.

'Eat,' he says gently. 'You've had nothing since morning.'

I take the sandwich. I sip the coffee. The scalding liquid burns my tongue and I'm shocked to feel it. I thought the news of Amit being brain dead would have anaesthetized me.

The tears that had dried now flow freely again.

I am reliving Ronit's death. Back then it had seemed like the end of the world. But I had to think of Amit. But now?

How will I live now without Amit, who just turned eighteen? Who had so much to offer? Who had yet to see the world?

I turn my anguished eyes towards Ravish. I've always been a creeper vine, clinging to something—someone—for support.

'Amit is gone,' he says softly. 'But he can help others live.

His eyes can still see. His heart can still beat. You may even meet those who receive his organs. See a part of him live on.'

Is that how he is consoling himself about Tanya's death? I wonder cynically.

I want to think it. But there's no time. Organs must be retrieved quickly. There are people waiting. People desperate for a heart, a kidney, a liver, eyes.

Some of them may be victims of the very same crash.

Ravish will take me to the doctor-in-charge. They'll need my permission to withdraw life support.

I am not a generous soul. Not really. But I know this is what Amit would have wanted. In any case, I have a lifetime to grieve.

16

Coming Home

There are days when I wish I never had to wake up. Today is one of those days. The repeated ringing of the bell wakes me up just minutes after I have drifted back to sleep. I get up grumpily. I have been suffering from insomnia ever since Rajesh passed away.

Who could it be? I wonder—and then I know. Only one person I know rings the bell repeatedly until one is forced to open the door.

Reema.

She has always been a rebellious child. Petulant. Sullen. Defiant. I rush to the door, grabbing the spectacles I had left on the table.

'Hi Reema, what a surprise,' I say, my smile warm.

Then I notice her eyes look puffy. I rub my glasses and put them on. Now I can see the purple bruise near one eye.

She has a black eye, bruises on her face and a cut on her lip. She is a battered wife.

I know all about battered wives. I counsel victims of domestic violence. I know that, statistically, about one-third of women admit to being subjected to it. I know it's a global phenomenon, not confined to India.

But this isn't about statistics. This is about my daughter.

She stands awkwardly before me, then says defiantly, 'Shashank has beaten me. I have left him for good.'

A packed suitcase stands behind her. Could eleven months of marriage fit into one suitcase? How empty her life must have been! I yearn to open my arms and hug her. But I hesitate. We have never been a demonstrative family. Truth be told, we have been a dysfunctional one, and Reema has always been an awkward child. I end up patting her back.

I know why I am hesitating. I remember the last time she was at this doorstep, brazen and bold. 'Ma, Papa, I have married Shashank,' she had declared.

It was a slap in our faces—just as she meant it to be. Rajesh had made it clear he did not approve of Shashank. Neither did I. For once, we were in unison. But she had gone ahead and married him anyway. Why? To defy us? To escape a house that had grown stifling? I do not know. And I did not believe she loved him.

Clichés swirl in my head. *You've made your bed, now lie in it. As you sow, so shall you reap.*

Did Reema provoke him? Was it the first time? Had he finally lost his patience?

I chide myself for even thinking such thoughts. I know no provocation justifies wife-beating. Rajesh never hit me, though we disagreed on almost everything.

I am known for my empathy. And yet, here I am—being judgemental.

Reema stands in the drawing room, awkward, while I fetch the first-aid kit.

'These wounds will heal,' she says sardonically, leaving the sentence incomplete.

I know what she means. I understand what she is trying to say. The silence between us grows.

Reema has always been difficult and moody. Or perhaps not always. Maybe it began after the catastrophic change in our lives—when Rohan drowned in the school swimming pool, while she was watching.

It was not her fault. She did not know how to swim. She raised the alarm, but by the time the lifeguard arrived it was too late.

That was the day she clung to me and cried her heart out. My eight-year-old daughter had been heartbroken. She had loved her elder brother deeply.

The tragedy broke us. Some families know how to cope with grief. Some do not. We drifted apart, immersed in our sorrow and guilt. And Reema blamed herself. She believed that if one of the children had to die, we would have preferred it to be her. She grew withdrawn and sullen, while Rajesh and I buried ourselves in work.

Now Reema has returned home, but forgets that things have changed. Rajesh is gone—and with him, our financial stability. His pension and my salary as a counsellor at an NGO are enough for me, but what about Reema's expenses? As far as I know, she's unemployed. Her visit won't be a short one. She may stay forever.

I remember bitterly that although she performed Rajesh's

last rites, she never bothered to find out how I was coping all by myself. That was the one time I had needed her. Ghaziabad isn't far from Delhi. She could have tried to mend things. Maybe she blamed me for Rajesh's heart attack. Or maybe she was too busy fighting her own battles.

'Let me make you a cup of tea,' I say after a while, as if a hot cup of tea is a panacea for all ills.

She sniffs.

I boil water, add milk, sugar, cardamom, cloves and ginger, and make masala chai—just the way she likes it.

'So, what happened?' I ask—not because I need to know, but because I am expected to ask.

'We fought,' she says, her voice weary.

'About what?' I ask. One must not rush a victim of domestic violence. She is expected to open up slowly.

The doorbell rings again. This time it is Amma, my massage woman. I sigh. A one-hour massage with sesame oil is just what I need. My aching calves will finally relax—and I'll get a reprieve from Reema's sad, sordid story.

I look at Reema.

'Go ahead,' she says.

I am about to usher Amma in when I notice someone hiding behind her: a young girl with a freshly scrubbed face.

'My granddaughter, Kajal,' Amma says proudly. 'Madam, you said you needed someone for the housework—Kajal can clean utensils, wash clothes, sweep, chop vegetables. You can pay her whatever you want.'

I close my eyes. Kajal is God-sent, now that Reema is back.

Amma spreads the mat on the drawing room floor and I lie down. Reema curls up on the sofa in a foetal position. She is clearly hurting.

As Amma's hands work rhythmically over my body, a sense of calm spreads through me.

Suddenly I ask, 'Didn't Kajal get married?'

I remember gifting her a saree.

'She did, but she came back.'

'Why?' I ask. 'Did her husband beat her?'

'No, no,' Amma says, shaking her head. 'But her in-laws made her work like a slave, and her brother-in-law had his eye on her. One night, when her husband was away, he entered her room at 1 a.m. It is better that Kajal is back with us.'

Amma leaves much unsaid—but I can read between the lines.

I'm surprised. I would have expected Kajal's family to send her back to her husband. Then I remember—it's Amma. She may be illiterate, but she is an empowered woman. After having two daughters, she underwent a tubectomy without informing her husband. And when he brought 'the other woman' into their house, Amma left—and began working as a masseuse.

She doesn't believe in the concept of *pati parameshwar*. She believes her granddaughter must never go back to that house.

'Thank God she is alive. What if she had killed herself?' Amma says simply. She then looks at me and says, 'Kajal will learn to fend for herself.'

The words echo in my mind. *Thank God she's alive,* I chant silently, looking at Reema—the surly, defiant girl neither Rajesh nor I ever hit, but who was tormented by her own demons. Perhaps all she ever wanted was our approval. And never got it.

We were partly to blame for her problems. Rajesh and I were two very different people, living under one roof, unable to turn our house into a home—not after Rohan died.

I feel a sudden urge to hold her. To cradle her as I did

when she was a baby. It was not her fault Rohan died. It is time to exorcise that ghost too.

I close my eyes, grateful that my unpredictable daughter has not done something foolish, and that she is still alive. Like Kajal, Reema will learn to fend for herself.

I get up, open my arms and call out, 'Reema.'

She jumps from the sofa and flies into my embrace. She becomes an eight-year-old once again.

'Welcome home,' I say—and I really mean it.

17

Dying Embers

I hate hospitals. I think everybody does—except perhaps new parents when they hear the cries of their newborn reverberating through the maternity ward. Hospitals are grim reminders that man is mortal, that life comes with no guarantees, and death comes for us all. I walked into City Hospital with a sense of dread. Although I did not consider my job as a public relations officer in a bank particularly glamorous, I was glad I did not have to sit behind a computer all day. As a bonus, I got to meet interesting people. But this was the first time I was doing something like this—visiting the almost dead. It was just a gesture from the bank's Managing Director, to show the organization cared for its employees and their families. I wished I had not been chosen as the messenger.

My husband Jayesh and I were to leave for Mussoorie that afternoon. I knew Jayesh would already be at the airport. He was a stickler for rules. If the airline asked passengers to report two hours before a flight, he would make sure we reached three hours early. He accounted for every eventuality—traffic jams, accidents, flat tyres—and planned accordingly. Sometimes his caution irritated me. At other times, I felt blessed.

The call from the bank that morning had ruined our plans. Then I felt a pang of guilt. I was going to see a woman who was hovering between life and death, and here I was, still thinking of my weekend getaway.

I entered the hospital and made my way to the Burns Unit. I cringed at the sight of patients being wheeled in on stretchers and felt almost guilty for being able-bodied and disgustingly healthy. It had everything to do with my jogging routine and an hour at the gym every evening. I donned a mask and put on the shoe covers, then entered the ward cautiously.

The woman I had come to see lay on the hospital bed with 90 per cent burns. She was burnt from head to toe. Her face looked like a macabre mask, reminding me of a brinjal roasted to a crisp, its burnt skin waiting to be peeled off. I flinched at the sight of her, then was instantly flooded with shame. Every minute that she was alive must be sheer agony. How could she endure it?

I had always prayed I might die in my sleep, unaware of my own passing. Jayesh had begged to differ—he wanted the chance to say goodbye.

'To each his own,' I had said when he told me.

This woman had no doubt she was about to die.

I wondered about the family she would leave behind. Perhaps she had imagined growing old with her husband, celebrating silver and golden anniversaries. Perhaps she had children. Maybe she was a career woman. I realized I knew nothing about her.

I looked at her closely. Had she once been fair or dusky? Was she beautiful? Then I scolded myself. Why was I thinking about appearances at a time like this?

Her eyes were open, and I could almost see life ebbing away. My own eyes welled up. She seemed to be looking straight at me. Was she trying to say something, or was I just imagining it?

I did not know what to say to her. I hoped she wouldn't misinterpret my silence. The nurse did not. She pressed my hand and said gently, 'The morphine deadens the pain. But when it wears off, the pain is unbearable.'

I stood there, head bowed, unable to watch her suffer, wondering just how long I had to stay before I could leave.

A man entered just then. He looked familiar. He must be Samarth Nath, the bank employee whose wife lay on the bed. I thought I had seen him at the branch once.

I watched his face pucker as he looked at her. He clenched his lips. The grief on his face made me ache. They must have spent years together. To see her in agony, before she died, must be excruciating.

A gasp escaped his lips. I realized he needed to be alone with her. I stepped out into the waiting area.

A little later, he came and sat beside me. His face crumpled, and he wept, childlike in his sorrow. I sat in awkward silence, not knowing what to do. Then suddenly I remembered why he looked familiar. I'd seen him once at Café Royale, near the bank's main branch. He had been with his wife. Her face had looked familiar too. Perhaps she worked in another branch. I remembered her laughing eyes, how she leaned towards him while talking, and how he bent closer to hear her. I had envied their ease. By comparison, Jayesh and I seemed jaded.

That was not true of course. Jayesh was the quiet kind, reserved and almost reclusive—that was part of what had drawn me to him. But sometimes I wished he would just throw back his head and laugh.

Samarth's voice broke into my thoughts. 'How could this happen? Who could have done this to her?'

I stayed silent.

'She was returning from her evening walk. Just before she reached our gate, someone poured petrol over her and lit a match. She could not see who it was. She screamed, but the road was deserted. She ran home, but no one was there.' He paused. 'I'd gone to the market. I wish I hadn't.'

I could already see the guilt that would haunt him. It began to gnaw at me too. She deserved so much more—a longer life, her share of happiness, perhaps a career, children. Not this.

Just then, two policemen approached the ward.

'They have come to take her dying declaration,' Samarth informed me.

That phrase—dying declaration—had such a terrible sense of finality to it. Samarth must have realized that there was really no hope.

No, I was wrong. He must have known that when he brought her to the hospital.

The policemen left after some time. The nurse came out a minute later and said, 'They took her dying declaration. She said she could not recognize him.'

So at least she was certain it was a man. It was a pity she had no idea who the perpetrator was. Perhaps he had worn a mask? Or it had been dark. Perhaps she had only glimpsed him briefly. Monsters like that deserved no mercy.

'You can see her now,' the nurse said.

Samarth hesitated. Perhaps he could not bear to see her like that. The nurse shrugged and began to walk away. Suddenly he got up and followed her. Five minutes later, he returned.

'She's gone,' he announced.

∽

I made it to the airport in time. Jayesh was waiting for me, his face drawn with resignation. It lit up when he spotted me, then clouded when he saw my tears. He realized that the woman I had gone to see was no more.

He opened his arms and held me. For Jayesh, that was a significant gesture. He was not demonstrative, and certainly not in public.

A month later, my colleague Mukund said casually, 'Samarth Nath has been arrested for the murder of his wife.'

'What!' I gasped. *How could it be?* I wondered. *He had been so in love with her.*

Mukund waved a newspaper at me. 'Don't you read the news? It's front page today.'

I looked down. The photo in the newspaper was not of the woman I had seen with Samarth at Café Royale.

Everything fell into place. So *that* woman—the one with the laughing eyes—wasn't his wife. She was probably a colleague. He must have been madly in love with her. That is why he murdered his wife.

Only a monster could have inflicted such agony. Why didn't he simply divorce her?

I wondered if his wife had guessed the truth—that it was her husband who had doused her in petrol, or arranged for someone else to do it. I hoped not. The pain of the burns would have been unbearable; to add the pain of betrayal to that would have been unthinkable.

The thought that I sat beside a murderer while his wife lay dying still gives me nightmares.

18

Cardiac Arrest

The day Jatin was to return from Canada I dreamt I had won the Booker Prize. I got up from the bed feeling rejuvenated.

Humming to myself as I dusted the house, I smiled at Sachin even when I saw him walk over to the dining table with his iPad. I served him his favourite breakfast—pancakes with a generous dollop of maple syrup.

'Hurry up and get dressed. We are going to the airport,' I said as soon as he had finished eating.

Sachin scowled, probably wondering why we all needed to be there.

'Show some enthusiasm—your father is returning after a year,' I admonished him.

My sister Latika nodded in agreement. She seldom disagreed with me. I wondered if it was a part of the corporate culture she had imbibed. We left for the airport, me humming under my breath.

'You sing so badly, Mom. Like a beggar singing at a railway station,' said Sachin, his voice droll.

I did not take umbrage at his remark. I was in too good a mood. I was looking forward to my husband's return.

Standing in the waiting area at the airport I glanced down at the blue and grey saree I was wearing, and hoped Jatin would like it. Perhaps I should have worn something more flamboyant, like the lilac dress Latika had on. She looked like a carton of Colgate toothpaste, I thought satirically.

Perhaps your profession begins to reflect on you, I mused.

Latika had joined Hindustan Unilever a year ago and had moved in with us when she relocated from Kolkata. Delhi was not considered safe for single women. I, on the other hand, taught Philosophy at a women's college. My taste in colour reflected my profession.

'Sachin, keep track of the flights. Papa's flight is due to arrive soon,' I said. Sachin was computer-savvy, while I was practically illiterate in such matters.

'Landed,' he said, checking the display.

I perked up, until he cast a dampener. 'It will take him twenty minutes to get off the plane and come through the aerobridge. Then immigration and baggage claim—another twenty-five minutes. Get real, Mom. You have a long wait ahead.'

Sachin was a prophet of doom. He believed whatever could go wrong, would. I shrugged.

'Forty-five minutes will pass.'

While we waited, I thought of Jatin's last phone call. He had sounded stressed. 'We need to talk,' he had said. That sounded ominous. But I was not worried. Jatin was always stressed. As a doctor, he should have learnt to avoid it. He was not only tense but also hyperactive. I sometimes wondered if he had undiagnosed ADHD. He often asked how I could sit in an armchair and ruminate, oblivious to the world.

'Philosophy, huh?' he said once before leaving.

'Well, it is better than selling toothpaste all your life,' I replied, taking a jab at Latika.

'It brings in the moolah,' Latika laughed good-naturedly.

'Not to say dental health isn't important,' Jatin added quickly, jumping to her defence.

'Look, Mom! There's Dad,' Sachin suddenly exclaimed.

I peered at the arrival gate but could not see him. I wondered if Sachin was long-sighted.

'He's got his phone out—he's clicking photos,' Sachin informed me.

Then I saw him—wearing his favourite blue and white checked shirt. I waved frantically. He waved back—and suddenly collapsed.

I wondered if he had slipped and fallen. As a crowd gathered around him, panic flared inside me.

I ran towards the gate. 'I am his wife,' I panted to the guard. He looked at my face and realized that this was not the time to enforce rules. He let me through. Sachin and Latika followed.

Someone was giving Jatin CPR—beating his chest, massaging it, repeating the sequence. He stopped after ten minutes and shook his head sadly. But he wasn't a doctor.

I later learnt CPR should be administered for thirty minutes. If a doctor had been present, Jatin might still have lived. Who knows.

'He died of cardiac arrest. Anything can trigger it. A shock. Great happiness. Great sorrow. Just anything.'

The words of the doctor, who had arrived at last, sounded well rehearsed. This is how he must explain it to all those who have lost their loved ones to cardiac arrest.

'Then why didn't I die of cardiac arrest?' I wanted to scream. But I said nothing. I just cried. The tears flowed unabated until Latika and Sachin guided me to a bench. I have no idea what formalities were done or how. I learnt later that Sachin, my fourteen-year-old, had taken charge.

Latika rested her hand on my shoulder. I sighed. Thank God for her. I don't know how I would have coped during this time without her. The meals would have gone uncooked, the clothes unwashed and the beds unmade because I would have been too busy crying.

I never realized how much I loved Jatin until he died. I never knew how much he loved me until the doctor said that Jatin had probably been so happy to see me after a year-long separation that it triggered his cardiac arrest. I was plagued by guilt. In a way, I was responsible for it.

'He died of happiness,' I told everyone who came for Jatin's cremation. They looked at me strangely, until Latika explained to them how he had died.

'He was waving excitedly. He was so happy to see me,' I said.

Sachin told me that I had absolutely no idea how forlorn I sounded.

I closed my eyes and thought of our fifteen years together. Over time, a distance had grown between us. I did not even know how it started.

Jatin had an explanation for it. 'Irreconcilable temperamental differences,' he had said.

I had been bewildered. We rarely fought.

If Latika had not moved in, the silence between us might have grown.

Funny how distance puts things in perspective. Problems that once felt gargantuan begin to look trivial. In Canada, Jatin must have realized that I was the perfect foil to him—laid-back and ready to take life as it came—leaving him free to chase his ambitions.

Perhaps he missed the coffee I made, the butter chicken I cooked and the apple crumble I baked. Perhaps distance had been necessary for us to realize how much we really meant to each other.

One evening, Sachin walked into the drawing room with Jatin's phone while I was making notes for my lecture; Latika was on her laptop.

'Mom, Dad's phone is password-protected. What is the password?'

'It is my birthday,' I said without looking up.

'Doesn't work—it's a new phone,' he said.

'Try his birthday, or yours.'

He tried both. Then, on a whim, he asked Latika hers.

'12 November 1990,' I said before she could reply.

The phone unlocked instantly.

Sachin scrolled through the gallery and then handed the phone to me, looking thunderstruck.

The last two photos Jatin had clicked were of Latika. I was not even in the frame.

Everything clicked into place suddenly. Jatin's terse, 'We need to talk,' the night before his departure; the sudden excitement when he saw us at the airport; the year Latika had spent in our house.

I had been blind. I had not known what was going on

under my own roof. What I had mistaken for banter between the two had been something more.

No wonder Jatin's heart burst with happiness on his arrival.

No wonder he collapsed.

I should have been angry with Jatin and Latika. After all, infidelity, whether physical or emotional, was betrayal. But all I felt was a tremendous sense of relief. A burden had lifted from my shoulders. I grieved for Jatin and always would, but I was no longer burdened with guilt.

I only hoped Latika was.

19

Memories of Happier Times

I am not psychic. So, when I got up that morning, I had no premonition that something untoward would happen to me. I returned from my walk at 7 a.m., opened the door and slumped into an armchair in the drawing room. A few minutes later, once I felt rested, I picked up the remote, switched on the TV and raised the volume. As the newsreader's voice filled the room, I relaxed. I was no longer alone. There was somebody else in the room, even if it was only a voice.

Half an hour later, I rolled out the yoga mat and began my practice. I only did simple exercises—pranayama and a few asanas. What I liked best, of course, was Yog Nidra, which came afterwards. I could close my eyes and fall into a deep slumber within minutes. But that day, I was restless. I could hear Siddhant shuffling around in the bedroom. I shrugged. Imagination can play such tricks on one.

Siddhant was gone. It had been a year since he died. I was

alone. I would have to live with this fact.

The phone rang. I did not need to look at my watch to know it was 8 a.m. The phone rang at the same time every day. Jayant must have set an alarm on his phone, a reminder that it was time to call Ma. Another box he could tick.

I wondered why I was feeling so aggrieved. Siddhant's words—'You will miss me when I'm gone'—began to echo in my head. I had never realized how true they were.

I switched off the television, picked up the phone and answered Jayant's perfunctory questions. 'How are you, Ma?'; 'All well?'; 'No health issues?' The conversation was over in two minutes. We no longer had anything to say to each other.

Afterwards, I fetched the leather diary containing my to-do list. I opened it and decided to visit my bank the next day.

'Chandni Chowk?' My niece Kavita's face puckered when she dropped in that evening. She had made it a point to visit me thrice a week since Siddhant passed away. Perhaps she felt I was her responsibility now, with Siddhant gone and Jayant in New York.

'What's wrong with you, Mausi?' she grumbled. 'Can't you withdraw money through your debit card?'

'That is what I always do, but I have to submit my life certificate to the bank,' I said, bridling a little.

'Oh,' she said, momentarily stumped. She was young. It was not her fault she did not know about such things. Then she retorted, 'Why don't you get your pension account transferred to the Munirka or JNU branch? That way, you wouldn't have to go all the way to Chandni Chowk.'

I smiled. 'I like going to Chandni Chowk. We are from Chandni Chowk, remember?'

She sniggered on hearing that. The young never quite see

the charm of the walled city. I could.

Every time I visited Chandni Chowk, I felt I had retrieved a slice of my childhood. I loved everything about it—the road that ran across Chandni Chowk to Fatehpuri, the gullies that branched into more lanes, leading to shops whose small entrances hid treasure troves within; Dariba Kalan, where jewellers sat in tiny rooms selling gold, polki work, kundan jewellery, diamonds, basra pearls; lanes draped in brocades, heavy Banarasi sarees, embroidered chiffons and fine tanchois; Nai Sarak, where books, fresh from the press, stood stacked from floor to ceiling as students, booklists in hand, hunted for textbooks.

∽

The next morning, I decided to take the bus to Chandni Chowk. I could have gone by autorickshaw, but when one lives on a family pension, one learns to be frugal. Besides, for me, time was no longer of the essence. I had all the time in the world.

'*Main aur meri tanhaai, aksar yeh baatein karte hain.*' I chuckled to myself, remembering the lyrics from *Silsila*. I had to accept the truth: I was alone.

I could not blame Jayant for not taking care of me. What did I expect—that he would pluck me from my DDA flat in Munirka and transport me to New York? That was impossible. He had a one-bedroom apartment in Manhattan and a live-in girlfriend, Sheela. I had met her when Jayant insisted I visit.

Sheela was nice. But after living with them for a month, sleeping on a couch in the living room, I realized I had overstayed my welcome. Her presence made me understand why Jayant did not feel the need to send me money. He probably needed the money for himself and Sheela. I would have to learn to live by myself—or sell my flat and move into assisted living, like Ashiana in Bhiwadi.

So lost was I in thought, I didn't even realize when the bus reached Chandni Chowk. After de-boarding, as I walked towards the bank, I paused at a *bedmi aloo* stall, where a cook rolled out balls of dough and dunked them into a karahi bubbling with hot oil. They puffed instantly. He flipped them expertly, then fished them out on a perforated dish to drain the excess oil. I was tempted to order a plate, to bite into the succulent potatoes and the lip-smacking gravy, topped with onions and green chillies. But I resisted. Chandni Chowk was full of culinary delights—the crispy parathas with curd and pickles in Paranthe Wali Gali, the mouth-watering *moong dal halwa* liberally sprinkled with *khoya*, almonds and chopped raisins, the giant *jalebis* fried in ghee.

Chandni Chowk was a foodie's delight, and if I gave in, there would be no stopping me.

My trip to the bank did not take as long as I had feared. Once my biometrics were done and the form signed, I was free to leave. I walked back, reminiscing. As I looked around, I realized so much had changed. Gone were the shops I had frequented when I lived in this area. New sweet shops had opened in their place.

'The old order changeth, yielding place to new,' I murmured. The old order was changing. One day, like Siddhant, I too would be gone.

By the time I reached the bus stop, I was beginning to feel despondent. *Is it possible to feel lonely in a crowd?* Perhaps it is.

A young boy came and sat beside me. He looked barely eighteen. He smiled, and his whole face transformed.

'Aunty,' he began hesitantly. 'May I call you Aunty?'

He was being polite. I could well have been his grandmother. I nodded.

'Where are you going?' he asked.

'Munirka,' I said reluctantly. I really did not like talking to strangers.

'What a coincidence! I am headed that way myself,' he said cheerfully.

'Where to?' I asked.

'JNU,' he said.

I looked at him again. He did not seem the JNU type. He looked more like someone who sold sarees. Or maybe hardware. I felt ashamed. I was typecasting him.

'Oh,' I said, unsure what else to say.

The bus arrived just then. The boy elbowed his way through the crowd, made way for me and slumped on to the last seat. I squeezed into the corner next to the window. I knew it would be a long journey. I had begun to feel hungry. I'd had only a sparse breakfast before I left. I took out my plastic tiffin box, which held two stuffed parathas, and gave him one—albeit a trifle reluctantly. I was not sure one paratha would be enough to assuage my own hunger. I wished I had eaten a plate of *bedmi aloo* after all.

He thanked me, flashing that charming smile once again. Then he took out two tetra packs of Frooti, put a straw in both, and gave me one.

'I don't drink Frooti,' I said, somewhat reluctantly. 'It is too sweet, and I am a borderline diabetic. Besides, this is November.'

'Today is my birthday, and I thought it called for a celebration,' he said, looking crestfallen.

'Happy birthday,' I wished him. 'How old are you... Err, I didn't get your name?'

'Raju,' he said, smiling again.

'Okay, I shall just have a bit,' I said, as I began sipping it.

ᔕ

I woke up feeling completely disoriented. My head hurt. It felt as though it might explode. *Where was I?* I wondered.

Without my glasses, my world was a blur. As I peered around, I recognized my bedroom, my bedside table and my glasses. Kavita rose from the armchair and walked towards me.

'Awake at last,' she said sardonically.

'At last? How long has it been?' I asked.

'This is the third day, Mausi,' she said.

'Have I been unconscious all this while?' I asked, alarmed.

'You were in and out of consciousness,' she replied. 'You got up to use the bathroom, had bowls of soup, but you were completely disoriented and your speech was slurred. The doctor warned us about this.'

'The doctor?' I echoed.

'Dr Rastogi, from the nearby dispensary,' she said.

I did not recall doctors making home visits any more. Then I saw Kavita preen. Clearly, she had used her clout.

Half an hour later, the doctor arrived.

'What is wrong with me?' I demanded.

'Did you eat or drink anything while you were in Chandni Chowk?' he asked.

I frowned and shook my head. 'Nothing except homemade parathas.' Then I remembered. 'And Frooti,' I added.

He sighed. 'This was a classic case of *dhatura* poisoning. It's fairly common,' he said. Then he turned to Kavita and asked, 'Has anything been stolen?'

She shook her head. 'I do not think so. Her mobile and cash were in her purse.'

I looked at my wrist. My thick gold bracelet was missing.

'My bracelet!' I screamed.

Kavita looked at me strangely. 'Were you foolish enough to wear that heavy gold *kada* when you went to Chandni Chowk?'

The doctor tut-tutted for a bit, realized he did not want to be drawn into an altercation, and left.

I promptly burst into tears—because I knew it would stop Kavita from giving me a proper dressing down. Ever since she had joined the police force a year ago, she had assumed the role of my guardian. But at that moment, I did not have the strength to listen to her tirade.

Kavita told me that when the bus I was on reached the last stop, the conductor had found me with my head slumped against the window. He tried to wake me, and when I did not respond, he raised the alarm. A nearby policeman, going through my belongings, found Kavita's number on my mobile and called her.

'We will have to lodge an FIR for your stolen bracelet,' Kavita muttered. 'You are lucky I am in the police.'

The policewoman who came to take my statement had a kindly face. She did not reprimand me like Kavita had. She only said gently, 'Stay safe, and please don't go to Chandni Chowk alone.'

∽

Three months later, I decided to go to Chandni Chowk once again. I rang up Kavita before leaving, and she blew her fuse.

'Do not go. You may not be so lucky this time,' she warned.

'I have urgent business at the bank,' I told her.

'What can be more precious than your life? Besides, it is a Saturday. The bank would be closed,' she said.

'It's the third Saturday. The bank will be open,' I retorted.

Once again, my work at the bank took barely twenty minutes. I decided not to dally and returned quickly to the bus stop.

Although it was not cold, there was a distinct chill in the air. I wrapped my shawl tightly around me. When I sat down on the bench, a young man sidled up beside me. I did not need to turn to guess who he was. Was Raju a regular at the bus stop? Just how many people had he conned? How come he had never been caught?

'Aunty ji, *kaisi ho*, how are you?' he asked, his voice mocking.

I shivered slightly, remembering Kavita's words: 'What can be more precious than your life?'

'Have you come to give me the other kada?' he laughed.

He then moved closer and pressed my hand warningly, in case I tried to shout. I took the pepper spray I held in my other hand and squeezed it into his eyes—just as I caught a glint of steel in his palm.

A knife. I shuddered. Why had I not listened to Kavita and stayed home? Why had I not anticipated that if I met Raju again, he would be armed?

'Stop,' I heard a voice behind me. A voice that was irritatingly familiar.

Kavita.

She twisted his arm expertly, making the knife fall. The constable with her—presumably from the Chandni Chowk thana—slid handcuffs around his wrists with practised ease, and then overturned Raju's carry bag, out of which rolled a collection of gold trinkets. I wondered how many innocent people he had robbed that day.

Kavita turned to the policewoman and said, 'Carry on. I am taking my aunt home.'

'It is lucky that today was my day off and I decided to follow you. Why did you go to Chandni Chowk again? Do you have a death wish?' Kavita bristled once we had reached home.

'I went to get my pension account transferred. No more trips to Chandni Chowk for me,' I replied equably.

20

Up in Smoke

Every man needs a sanctuary. I was glad that I had found mine. It was the balcony behind my study. I had forgotten it even existed, hidden as it was behind a thick blue curtain. I remembered it only when Vanya looked at me with a pained expression after catching me blowing cigarette rings in the drawing room.

'You are covered in smoke,' she said, visibly hurt.

'I know, I know,' I replied, hurriedly stubbing it out in deference to her wishes.

'You do know smoking kills, don't you?' she asked.

'Darling, I do,' I said sarcastically. 'The warning on the cigarette packet says so, and believe me, I am not illiterate.'

She flinched, as though I had struck her. Words can wound, I realized, yet I felt no remorse. I hated her nagging about smoking. *No*, I corrected myself, *I hated her nagging me*.

I knew she was worried about me. She could not help it; she

was a worrier. She worried about my cholesterol, my triglycerides, my blood sugar. She worried endlessly. She kept herself fit. Jogged three kilometres every day, even in winter. Practised yoga without fail. She had begun to lose weight as a result.

'At this rate, you'll disappear,' I had told her, laughing.

Vanya had always been slim.

She had smiled and replied, 'Why don't you join me while jogging?'

I knew what was coming next.

'You need to exercise; you lead a sedentary life.'

'Wearing a jacket? No thank you. I have my treadmill,' I retorted, quick to cut her off.

'And it is gathering dust,' she replied lightly.

'You worry too much about me,' I said.

'I can't help it,' she murmured. 'You know my father died when he was just fifty—'

'Of a heart attack,' I completed the sentence. I could recite the story backwards. I had heard it so many times. Her father, a chain-smoker, had a heart attack at thirty-six and died at fifty. He used to smoked incessantly, with no concern for himself, his wife or his only daughter.

'A curtain of smoke hung in our drawing room,' said Vanya, 'but Papa kept smoking. He had a smoker's heart attack. The angiography showed his left artery was fully blocked. Single-vessel disease, due to his incessant smoking. Bypass surgery was not required, since only one artery was affected, so he was put on a regimen of medication, diet and exercise. The attack brought us some respite, because he was forced to quit, but the damage had already been done. He still died young.'

I clicked my tongue in mock sympathy, and she seemed comforted.

On that December afternoon, I stood shivering on the balcony, despite the thick cardigan I wore. The Qutb Minar loomed in the distance—a majestic sight. At 72.5 metres, it is the tallest brick minaret. Although it is attributed to Qutb ud-Din Aibak, its completion was actually the work of his son-in-law Iltutmish.

I stood admiring the Minar, feeling drawn to it, as usual. While we could glimpse it from the drawing room as well, the view from the balcony allowed me to appreciate it in all its glory. Even now, surrounded by bare trees, it served as a source of inspiration for my historical romances.

Although romance is often considered a woman's domain, some men excel in it—Nicholas Sparks, for instance. I preferred old-world romance. I wrote about kings and queens and concubines; fortresses with moats; warriors charging on horseback, flashing swords and hurling war cries. Thankfully, my publisher liked my work.

I returned to the drawing room, opened my laptop, lit a cigarette and got down to work. Vanya walked in just then and began to sniff.

Just like a fox terrier, I thought. Her eyes bore into mine. I quailed.

'My publisher is pressing me to submit the manuscript… I need to smoke,' I said before she could say anything.

'Don't,' she said, then abruptly left the room.

I sighed. She had disrupted my creative flow. The words froze. I shut the laptop and returned to bed, my mind seething.

When I had first met Vanya, I had enjoyed her concern. I wondered when that concern had soured into suffocation.

I wished we had a child, someone for her to dote on, smother with care and affection, distract her from me. Then she would have left me alone. I wished she had not given up her job at the bank. She had not realized then that being a homemaker would leave her with long, empty hours.

Her concern made me feel trapped.

∽

A few days later, she caught me smoking in the study.

'What is it now?' she asked, her voice heavy with despair.

I resisted the urge to retort, 'It's really none of your business.' Instead, I counted to ten and replied, 'I have to make a presentation before the chairman of my bank the day after tomorrow. It is very important. Creative writing feeds my ego, but my bank job keeps the stove burning. You know ideas do not flow unless I smoke.'

'You must be joking,' she said, eyes wide. 'Not everyone smokes. I do not.'

I shrugged. She did not need to. She was just a homemaker, with maids to help her with the housework. I was the one who faced professional stress.

'I know what happened to my father,' she said again, shuddering. 'Our house was always filled with smoke. He smoked, never caring about his health, or ours for that matter. He needed no excuse. He smoked when he was happy, when he was sad or when he wanted to celebrate. Look what happened to him.'

I smiled. 'Churchill smoked cigars throughout his life, led England to victory in the Second World War and died at ninety.'

'One can't win an argument with you,' she said, almost petulantly.

That night, I worked on my presentation, lighting one cigarette after another. Seeing the glowing tip made me feel warmer, though I still shivered. We have no central heating in India, and the radiator was inadequate. Perhaps a draught was sneaking in through the windows. I went to check—they were tightly shut. I should have known. Vanya was never careless with such things. The temperature must have dropped suddenly. Perhaps it had snowed in Shimla. Or Kashmir.

I shivered again.

I was making a presentation on cybersecurity, one of the most serious threats banks currently face. With more and more transactions moving online, it had become critical to develop robust systems that could withstand breaches and protect data. My presentation had to be flawless—after all, I would be presenting it before both the managing director and the chairman. I only wished Vanya could understand, instead of growing increasingly paranoid.

Suddenly, I was seized by a paroxysm of coughing. I tried to control it, but could not. Just then, Vanya walked into the room, wrapped in her woollen dressing gown.

'What happened, Vivek?' she asked, her face puckered.

'Nothing, it's just a cough,' I said, even as I wheezed and struggled to catch my breath.

'I'm taking you to the hospital,' she said, her tone brooking no argument.

I gave in. She even rang my friend Sudeep, asking him to accompany us.

'Why trouble him—drag him out in this cold?' I asked.

'He will survive,' she replied curtly.

As we waited for the doctor, I began to sweat profusely. A tightness gripped my chest. I wondered if this was a heart attack—one of the very things Vanya had warned me about time and again.

I found myself praying silently, bargaining with God. *Please let me not die young. I have so much to live for.*

'You smoke,' said the doctor, almost casually, as he began to examine me. It did not take a genius to deduce that—I reeked of tobacco. He ordered an ECG.

When the report came, he said, 'Your heart is fine. It looks like a severe case of bronchitis. We'll keep you overnight for observation, just to rule out anything else.'

'Just another way to make money,' I muttered, once my coughing subsided and the fear had receded. With the diagnosis delivered, I began to relax.

The next morning, as the discharge formalities were being prepared, the doctor glanced at me over his glasses and said, 'I would advise you to give up smoking.'

I looked at Vanya, expecting her to smile in vindication. Instead, I saw a spasm of pain cross her face. She winced. Why was she wincing?

Then she began to gasp.

'Doctor, my wife is in pain,' I called out.

Vanya's voice came in a strained whisper. 'I think it's a heart attack.'

The doctor reached her just as she was about to collapse.

Heart attack? At forty? I could not believe it. I had heard oestrogen protects women against heart disease during their childbearing years. We had no children, but still—wasn't she too young?

Everything shifted that instant. Vanya was the priority now.

While I got discharged, Vanya was now in urgent need of care.

She was taken for tests. The doctor returned after some time and declared, 'Her ECG is normal. This wasn't a heart attack.'

'Thank God,' I sighed in relief, shutting my eyes. I did not want the tears to spill. Men do not cry—at least, strong men do not. It is a sign of weakness.

Vanya was kept under observation. I remained in the hospital with her, forgetting all about the cybersecurity presentation.

Heavens wouldn't fall if I don't deliver the presentation; it can always be rescheduled, I told myself. I had already applied for leave.

Another doctor arrived. 'Her chest X-ray shows fluid in the lungs,' he said.

'Pleurisy?' I asked. I had it once—fluid in the lungs. 'Or it could be TB,' I added. Luckily, both were treatable.

I smiled at Vanya. 'God has been merciful,' I muttered as I held her hand.

The next day, when the doctor arrived again, his face was grave. 'It is neither pleurisy nor TB,' he said.

I thought he would be pleased to deliver that news. Instead, he added, 'We need to run more tests.'

When he returned with the reports the following day, he looked solemn.

'What is it?' I asked.

He took me outside and handed me the report. I blinked at it. The words blurred. I was unable to read them clearly. I was forty-five now; perhaps it was time to accept I needed reading glasses.

I held the paper farther away.

Adenocarcinoma.

I was not mistaken the first time I had read the report.

'Lung cancer. Stage IV. It is metastatic,' said the doctor quietly.

Then, noticing me looking blankly at him, he explained,

'It has spread. We need to do a PET scan to confirm the full extent.'

'Lung cancer? But she doesn't smoke,' I protested.

'One doesn't have to smoke. There are multiple causes of lung cancer,' he said. Then he narrowed his eyes at me and added, 'She may not smoke, but you do.'

He did not have to say more. I knew. Vanya had been exposed to passive smoking most of her life, in fact, since her birth. I knew that both her father and I were responsible for her cancer. She had lost weight recently, but I thought it was simply due to her daily jogging. She coughed occasionally, but I had mistaken it for allergies. I had been so self-absorbed that I had missed all the warning signs.

'How long does she have?' I asked. It was the question I had never imagined uttering.

'I can't say definitively until we run the PET scan,' he replied, but he was stalling.

'Just tell me.'

He hesitated, then said, 'Three years. At most.'

I knew he was being generous.

Vanya died six months later.

I gave up smoking the day we got her diagnosis. I have not touched a cigarette since.

21

Roosevelt Island

'Serenity has a new name—Roosevelt Island in New York,' I said to myself.

I stood by Roosevelt Island's seawalk railing, looking at the East River, as the wind blew my hair away from my face. This was my favourite place on the island. Standing there, I could see the Manhattan skyline. I loved looking at the skyscrapers. I could even see the United Nations Secretariat. I watched the boats cruise along the river and gulped the fresh air—so different from the polluted Delhi air. I was lucky to be in New York. After all, how many people in the world had a chance to visit it?

I turned around and smiled as I saw a man on a bench, sketching furiously in his sketchpad. Suddenly he looked up, and my smile wavered. He was brown-skinned. Perhaps he was Indian or from somewhere in the Indian subcontinent. I smiled again, but he looked through me. For a moment I was disconcerted, but then I realized he was not being deliberately rude—his eyes were fixed ahead, perhaps focusing on the scene before him. He was an artist. My fingers itched to snatch the sketchpad from his hands and draw the view before me. Why hadn't I brought my painting materials from India? Now I would have to ask my bhaiya and bhabhi for them. *Maybe*, I thought wistfully, *we could go shopping for some*.

I returned to my apartment and shut the door behind me. As soon as I entered the drawing room, I began to feel claustrophobic. The flat was small, and I longed for the big open spaces I was used to in India. I yearned for charcoal and paper, oil paints, linseed oil and turpentine. I missed my easel, the smell of turpentine on my overalls, the aquamarine smudges on my kurta, the streak of Prussian blue—my favourite colour—across my face.

I ran a comb through my hair, locked the apartment and walked to my niece and nephew's school to pick them up.

As they walked slowly beside me, looking a little wary, I realized that it takes a great deal of effort to win a child's trust.

'Rice, dal anyone?' I asked brightly once we returned home.

My niece, Nina, pouted. 'Chicken nuggets,' she said.

'Same,' said Abhay laconically.

I microwaved the chicken nuggets obediently, served the children, put away their school bags and meekly tried to dissuade them from playing with their iPads.

After lunch I dozed off. I woke up an hour later and realized it was time to take them out to play. After that, I got busy preparing dinner. We Indians liked home-cooked meals—rice, dal, vegetables, chicken and rotis. I was exhausted after cooking the meal.

Deepa Bhabhi and Varun Bhaiya arrived after some time,

smiled mechanically at me and went into the children's room. Later that night, Deepa Bhabhi came into the drawing room—where I slept on the sofa-cum-bed—and put her arms around me.

'Hemant's death is so heartbreaking. I am sure you must be devastated,' she said.

It had been three years since my husband Hemant died. Varun Bhaiya and Deepa Bhabhi had not been able to come to India at the time. Hemant was just a memory now. Deepa Bhabhi did not know that when one has been married for just five months, one hardly knows one's husband. And when he passes away in an accident, what one mourns isn't so much a husband but a young man whose life was cut short in its prime.

Later that night, I went to the closet Deepa Bhabhi had cleared out for my clothes and crossed a day off the calendar I had kept there.

The next day, after waking the kids and giving them cereal and milk for breakfast, I walked down with them to their school and then returned to my favourite spot. A cloak of tranquillity seemed to drop over my shoulders. I decided to make the most of it. I knew it would not last forever. I revelled in the beauty of the scene before me. After a while, I noticed that the artist I had seen the day before was once again on the bench, sketching furiously. I went and sat down beside him.

'Hi, may I see what you are sketching?' I asked.

He raised his eyebrows, then shoved the sketchbook towards me. Looking at his sketches, I realized he was a maestro. He must have heard my inward breath.

'These are fabulous. You are in a class by yourself,' I gushed.

'You really think so?' he asked, a trifle wistfully. 'Do you sketch too?'

'I did when I was in Delhi,' I said.

'You are from Delhi?' Animation crept into his voice, and his demeanour changed. Suddenly he became friendly. I realized we were two lost souls in New York.

As I returned to the apartment, it struck me that I had not stepped out of Roosevelt Island since I'd arrived.

'There's enough time,' Varun Bhaiya had said when Deepa Bhabhi suggested taking me to Manhattan over the weekend. 'She is here for six months. We can take her around New York some other time.'

I knew why I was in New York for six months. It was not Varun Bhaiya's brotherly love that had plucked me from my home in Model Town, Delhi, and brought me here. The truth was, Deepa Bhabhi was doing a short-term course in journalism after years as a stay-at-home wife. Childminders were frightfully expensive in New York. The crèche in Roosevelt Island was fully booked, and there was a long waiting list.

For Varun Bhaiya, bringing me here was the cheaper option. Of course, they did not say so. They pretended I needed a change after the tragedy that had shattered my life. I wanted to tell them that three years is enough time to grieve. Of course, everyone else in the family was grateful to Varun Bhaiya for his gesture. Fortunately, getting a US visa hadn't been a problem.

'Are you a painter by profession?' I asked the artist on the bench.

He laughed. 'It is just a hobby, though I had wanted to make it my profession. I make my living crunching numbers at a bank.'

'That's soul-destroying,' I said.

He laughed again. 'You're candid. That's refreshing.' He told me his name was Rohan.

'Don't ask me what it means—I don't know,' he said, chuckling.

'I won't,' I smiled. I told him my name was Naina, and he said, 'That is appropriate. You have almond eyes.'

The way he said it made me blush.

Then he asked me if I had seen the Roosevelt Memorial. I confessed that I had not been outside Roosevelt Island. 'Roosevelt Memorial is on the island itself,' he reassured me. We walked to the memorial, and I was astounded by the beautiful surroundings. The statue of Franklin D. Roosevelt was magnificent, as was the verdant green around it. We sat and talked about FDR and his role during the Second World War. Then Rohan began sketching the memorial while I gazed at the beauty around me.

After that, we began to meet every day. We did not speak much. He would be busy sketching while I just sat and watched. At times, I sketched as well.

'You have a lot of promise,' he said when he saw my work. 'You just need to practise.'

I glowed upon hearing his words. They bolstered my confidence. I decided to take up painting seriously once again.

About a month later, he said, 'I am going away the day after tomorrow. I came to see if there were any takers for my art, but my sister Monali would not introduce me to any of her friends. She is a doctor. There were times I was out sketching and she forgot to hand me the house keys before leaving, locking me out. I wonder if she suspects I will steal something from her. I am a senior manager in a nationalized bank, you know.'

'Oh God! What did you do the whole day?'

'Oh, I always keep a pack of sandwiches with me. And I bought myself coffee from Starbucks,' he said. Although he did not say anything else, I could hear the hurt in his voice.

'Before I leave this place, I would like to take you out for lunch,' he told me.

I hesitated, unsure. 'I am afraid I can't. I have to pick up my niece and nephew from school every day.'

He smiled and said, 'Then we will go to the Japanese restaurant on Roosevelt Island itself.'

Someone could see us and tell Varun Bhaiya or Deepa Bhabhi about it, I thought nervously. And then I said to myself, *What the hell, I am an adult. Why shouldn't I do as I please?*

'Have you been to a Japanese restaurant before?' he asked suddenly.

I shook my head.

'Well, there's always a first time,' he said.

The next day he took me to the restaurant on the island. I walked beside him, which made a welcome change. I remembered that I had always walked behind Hemant in India. Rohan introduced me to sushi and tempura, edamame and miso soup—foods I had never tasted before. I found everything delicious, perhaps because I was with Rohan. I wished the afternoon would stretch on.

Rohan asked me about myself—not merely out of politeness, but as though he genuinely wanted to know. It was then that I told him about Hemant.

'You are a widow?' he exclaimed, his eyes wide with shock. 'You look so young! I thought you were unmarried.'

He left me at my apartment building and smiled wryly.

'I have to leave now. I must look for a washroom—Monali's locked me out again!'

'Come inside; you can use the one in our flat,' I said.

'Are you sure?' he asked hesitantly.

I nodded and led him inside the flat. When he came out,

he walked towards me and gently took me into his arms. My heart began to pound loudly. I wondered if he could hear it too. Hemant had passed away three years ago. I had almost forgotten what a man's touch felt like. As he looked into my eyes, my lips parted of their own volition. For once I didn't care what anyone thought.

ᔕ

A friend of Deepa Bhabhi came to our house a month later. She introduced me as her widowed sister-in-law, and the friend murmured words of sympathy.

'What do you do?' she asked me.

'I paint,' I said, almost apologetically. I wished I could have said that I was a software engineer or an oncologist instead.

'So does my brother, Rohan. Perhaps you saw him sketching on the island,' she said.

I looked at her with interest. So, she was Monali—Rohan's sister, the one who often locked him out of the house.

'Yes,' I said, nodding vigorously. 'We are both painters. We have much in common.'

'I hope not too much,' she said laconically.

I was intrigued by her silence. Perhaps she sensed my curiosity, because she started saying, 'My brother,' and then stopped. A little later, she continued. 'My brother—I hate to admit—came to New York only to get away from a scandal in India.'

Seeing the look of curiosity on my face, she said, 'He was about to marry a girl when one of the countless girls he had been with appeared with a baby, which she claimed was his. Naturally, his engagement broke, and to get away from the scandal, he came to New York. I knew that no girl was safe around him, which is why I did not introduce him to my friends. In fact, I often kept the house locked so that he could not bring women home.'

I was stunned. Rohan had told me something entirely different.

'He would not be interested in you if he knew you were a widow. You are not his type anyway,' she concluded dismissively.

'You are right. I am not,' I said.

After she left, I thought of the day he had come home. A shiver ran down my spine as I remembered the moment he took me in his arms, and that heavenly hour in the bedroom. He had transported me to a world of delight. I had thought it was because of his feelings for me. Now, I knew better.

I smiled as I remembered the interlude. It did not matter that he was only looking for a good time. I had not expected a lasting relationship anyway. We had been two consenting adults.

The tryst with him had made me acknowledge my needs—both physical and emotional. I was not a ball to be tossed among relatives. Rohan had shown me that I had my entire life ahead of me, to do as I pleased. He had taught me a lesson—one I was unlikely to forget.

I was disappointed, no doubt, by Monali's revelations, but not truly heartbroken. I knew I would recover.

22

Angel of Mercy

I suffer from claustrophobia. At least I think I do. Confined spaces scare me. I like wide open spaces. My favourite spot in our house is the balcony. I love sitting in it and soaking in the sun.

The sunlight lit up my grandfather's face; he was seated beside me. His weather-beaten face had character. I looked at the deep furrows on his forehead and smiled. He had earned them—the furrows, the wrinkles and the laugh lines—which he had acquired standing in harsh terrain, supervising the construction of buildings. He had retired as Chief Engineer, Public Works Department. Grandpa had loved his work. I hoped that when I chose a profession, I would love it just as much.

I was young, just seventeen, and could not make up my mind about what I wanted to be. 'An astronaut like Sunita Williams, a bestselling author like J.K. Rowling or a famous painter like Anjolie Ela Menon.'

‘Why not settle for something a little less esoteric—like a doctor, a lawyer or a civil servant,’ remarked my brother Mihir, as he drew up a chair and sat down beside us.

I flushed. I had not realized I had spoken out loud.

The maid came and placed a tray with three mugs of tea and a plate of digestive biscuits before us. As I picked up my mug, Grandpa spoke.

‘Let her be, Mihir. Let her dream. She’s young.’

‘She is seventeen, Dadaji—old enough to know what she wants,’ said Mihir Bhaiya. ‘Last week she was not sure whether she wanted to be a ballet dancer, a scientist or a nun, and the week before that she wavered between being a paratrooper, a deep-sea diver and a pirate.’

He sounded exasperated.

Dadaji laughed. ‘She does it only to annoy you, Mihir. You get ruffled so easily,’ he said.

I smiled at Dadaji. He was right. Mihir was serious and had been so since childhood. He had decided very early that he wanted to be a doctor. He had no grandiose dreams like being an astronaut. He wanted to heal people and save lives. My dreams were more extravagant. They ranged from the sublime to the ridiculous. I knew I drove Mihir Bhaiya mad with my natter.

Grandpa encouraged me in my dreams, even though they changed every fortnight. That was why I loved him. I loved him even more because he had given us a home when Mummy and Papa passed away from dengue, within one week of each other. The loss of my parents was a tragedy of monumental proportions. I could not overcome my grief. Time, everyone says, is a great healer. I can vouch that it’s untrue. I still cry myself to sleep most nights.

I hadn't known my grandfather very well before that, although he visited from time to time. We had been a close-knit family, and Dadaji had remained an outsider. My parents' deaths changed all that.

Dadaji had built a sprawling bungalow for himself. It had a large drawing-cum-dining room, four bedrooms, a study, a terrace and a huge lawn. It was a big house for someone who lived alone.

'I had hoped my son and daughter-in-law would live with me, but they had other plans,' he had said quietly when I asked him about it.

He did not say much, but from the little that he did, I gathered that my mother had been responsible for keeping my grandfather away from the family, even after Dadi passed away.

Dadaji was sprightly for his age. Every morning he went to the nearby park for a walk. I could hear laughter coming from the park and guessed he was part of the laughter club.

The rest of the time, he read the newspaper and books or watched television. Sometimes his friends came over for a game of rummy or bridge.

Thankfully, Grandpa had no major illnesses except diabetes, although he was seventy-five. That is why, when he fell ill, it took us by surprise.

One morning, as he returned from his walk and sat down for tea, he suddenly grimaced and then seemed unable to move. When he tried to speak, his voice sounded guttural.

'Ram Singh!' I shouted to the cook, urging him to come immediately. I rang up Mihir Bhaiya, who asked me to bring Dadaji to the hospital right away.

I booked an Uber, and though the drive took less than half an hour, the journey seemed inordinately long. I sat in the waiting room with Ram Singh, waiting for Mihir Bhaiya to tell me what was wrong.

When Mihir Bhaiya came, he informed me that Dadaji had suffered a stroke. The right side of his body was paralysed.

He remained in hospital for a month.

Mihir Bhaiya engaged a full-time male attendant to look after Dadaji. When Dadaji returned home, he wanted to be wheeled into the balcony every day. There was usually a faraway look in his eyes, as if he were missing the life he had led before the stroke.

One day, as I sat in the balcony with him, I found him getting agitated. I could not understand what he was saying. By the time the attendant came, I saw he had wet his pyjamas. The man who had been so proud had turned into a child. I shuddered and ran inside.

'How can you behave like this? He may have had a stroke, but he is not an imbecile. He understands everything,' Mihir Bhaiya thundered when he saw me. 'All he needs are adult diapers. I wonder why I did not think of it earlier.'

I suppose one gets used to illness after a while. I was able to manage, thanks to Dadaji's attendant, Keshav.

Then one day, Keshav came to me. 'I am afraid I have to leave. My wife needs me.'

'What about us?' I hollered.

'Please ask Mihir Bhaiya to speak to the agency. They will send a replacement,' he said.

'What if your replacement is not as good as you? You cannot leave us in the lurch like this. We have a one-year contract with the agency,' I argued.

But Mihir Bhaiya turned out to be more understanding than I was. He spoke to the agency, and that is how Sujit came to work for us.

Sujit had become available because the patient he had been attending had passed away—Mihir Bhaiya's friend Prashant's father, whom I knew as Tewari Uncle.

Sujit had the kindest eyes I had ever seen. He was very tender-hearted. I observed the gentleness with which he treated Dadaji. Tears filled his eyes when he noticed there was not much improvement in Dadaji's condition, even after the physiotherapy sessions.

As Sujit watched Dadaji try to raise his hand and fail, he did not hesitate to let his tears fall.

'The last gentleman I was with died three days ago,' he said sadly. 'I had worked there for just six months. The one before that died eight months after I started.'

'This happens with geriatric care,' consoled Mihir Bhaiya.

Two days later, Dadaji collapsed after lunch. We rushed him to the hospital, but it was soon over.

That evening, Mihir Bhaiya said, 'Sanyukta, it will come as a shock to you, but Sujit has been accused of murder.'

'Murder?' I exclaimed.

'Yes. You know Sujit was working in Tewari Uncle's house when Tewari Uncle's blood sugar dropped dangerously and he died. Prashant had suspicions about the death and insisted on a post-mortem.'

'The blood sugar level of diabetics tends to fluctuate, especially at night. There is always a danger that if that happens, the person may sink rapidly,' I said.

Mihir Bhaiya laughed and said, 'You are talking to a doctor, Sanyukta. What you are saying has been gleaned from books. What I know is first-hand. Tewari Uncle's blood sugar was being recorded daily by Prashant. It could have dipped so low only if someone had injected him with a very high dose of insulin.'

'Really?' I asked, bewildered.

'Yes,' said Mihir Bhaiya emphatically. 'They have arrested Sujit. He is being interrogated.'

The next day, he told me, 'Sujit has confessed to murdering five of his patients. Of course, he does not call it murder. He sees himself as an angel of mercy. He has probably modelled himself on Charles Cullen of West Orange in New Jersey, who is estimated to have murdered 400 patients—29 confirmed.'

I shuddered at the thought of having lived with a murderer for a few days.

The next evening, when Mihir Bhaiya returned from the hospital, he looked at me strangely.

'What is the matter?' I asked.

'Sujit confessed to the deaths of five people. But he says Dadaji wasn't one of them.'

I heaved a sigh of relief. 'Then he must have died a natural death.'

'I agree. However, I had already ordered a post-mortem after Prashant told me about the circumstances of Tewari Uncle's death. I am waiting for the report.'

Then he asked casually, 'By the way, you gave Dadaji his insulin shot yesterday, since Sujit had gone out at lunchtime, didn't you?'

'Yes, I did,' I replied, my voice calm.

His eyes darkened with suspicion. I stared back, my face expressionless.

Sujit was not the only person who viewed himself as an angel of mercy. I did as well.

Ever since Mihir Bhaiya had told me about the concept of 'assisted death' prevalent in Scandinavian countries, I had become a great believer in it. I truly believe in death with dignity. I knew that was what Dadaji had been trying to tell me all along. But I did not think Mihir Bhaiya would understand.

I would have to do something about him. And quickly.

23

The Murder I Solved

I wonder what I hate more—my fractured leg or the lockdown. I cannot make up my mind. I hate both with a slow, burning anger. Even if the lockdown ends, I will still be immobile for another month and a half. So maybe it is the fracture.

Nothing ever happens. We are trapped inside this 1,200-square-foot house. There is no space to move. Not that I can move anyway—not without crutches, and that does not count. Even the air smells stale. It reeks of cigarette smoke and whisky. Of course, no cigarette has been lit in the house for two weeks, no whisky has been drunk, and I use the air purifier daily—but you get my drift.

There are houses like those of my neighbours, brightly lit, with curtains pulled open, sunshine streaking in, where people perform pranayama after waking up and padmasana afterwards.

Then there are houses like mine, cloaked in thick dark curtains with lining. Not a single window in our house has been opened for two weeks, thanks to the coronavirus pandemic.

I yell to my mother, 'Open the windows. You know that coronavirus is not airborne.'

'You never know,' Ma says quickly.

'Every television news channel says so,' I persist.

'They could be wrong,' she argues.

'The WHO and the ICMR also say so,' I tell her.

'Doctors are not infallible. They could be wrong,' she replies.

In our house, only one person is right. My mother.

I never thought I'd say this, but I miss Abhishek Bhaiya. He is dominating—no, domineering—rude and has a macabre sense of humour, but Ma is afraid of him. She adores him of course.

Abhishek Bhaiya is stranded in Delhi, where he went for a meeting—two days later, the lockdown was announced. All flights were cancelled, and trains as well. So while he is stuck in our New Delhi house, we are stuck in his Mumbai flat.

I wonder who has it worse. I concede—it may be Bhaiya. He cannot cook, and takeaways are not delivering. Just how long can someone live on Maggi noodles and omelettes?

Mere paas Ma hai, I giggle to myself—not that she's much help.

This morning Ma came to me and asked, 'What would you like for breakfast? Cornflakes and milk or muesli?'

I made a face. 'Aloo ka paratha,' I said.

She looked at me in consternation. 'How can you even ask?'

'French toast?' I wheedled. I was not asking for the moon. It is not that she can't cook—she can. She just wants the groceries to last as long as possible.

In the end, she brought me one boiled egg and two pieces of toast, with a sliver of butter on each. She is trying to save the butter as well. I can order groceries online—they count as essential services—but she's the one who has to go down to the lobby to pick them up.

She looks quaint in her mask and gloves whenever she leaves the apartment. She is scared. She carries a tissue to press the lift buttons—outside and inside—making sure she touches nothing directly. She returns with a martyred look, dumps the jute bag on the floor, peels off the gloves and scrubs her hands vigorously with hand sanitizer, though she has not touched anything with bare hands. We have hot water and Dettol liquid soap in the bathroom, but maybe the sanitizer feels more reassuring. Who knows.

After some time, I pull out the drone from under my bed, hobble on to the balcony next to my room on my crutches, and fly it—the remote in my hand. It buzzes around like a giant bumblebee, gliding up and down past buildings, two floors up, two floors down. I have seen the pictures. I have learnt to retrieve them.

I wonder whether the drone has fun. I saw a drone in *3 Idiots*, and also in *Uri*. Flying the drone is just something I do to while away the time.

There is a TV in my room, but I don't have Netflix or Amazon Prime—just cable, which bores me. We have all the platforms—Netflix, Prime Video, Disney+ Hotstar, SonyLIV—on the TV in the drawing room. But Ma won't let me hobble there on crutches. She insists I need bed rest.

Abhishek Bhaiya is mean. He could have bought an Amazon Fire Stick for my TV too. I could order one online, but I do not know the passwords for the streaming apps. He wanted me to study. And to be fair, he hadn't anticipated my fracture. He did not think I would slip in the lobby of our building.

I wanted to sue the housing society, but Bhaiya wouldn't hear of it. At times, I wonder if he is my brother or my enemy. I am glad my leg broke before the lockdown. Ma would have been hysterical if she had had to take me to hospital during it.

The drone is a different story altogether. Maybe it will catch something interesting—like the day that young woman drowned in the swimming pool, just outside our apartment block. I had not known about drones then. I wish I had.

The woman had gone for a late-night swim. Or maybe an early-morning one—I'm not sure. A morning walker had found her body floating in the pool. Her death caused a sensation. The police were flummoxed. I empathized with them. Anyone would be—our society has thirteen apartment blocks, each with twenty-eight floors and six flats on each floor. The numbers are mind-boggling.

Soon afterwards, the lockdown began and the investigation became sluggish.

∽

I am dozing in the afternoon when there is a knock on the door. Mother comes to my room, her lower lip trembling just a little. Maybe I imagined it. Ma is tough—at least when she wants to be. During the lockdown, no one comes to our house regularly except the BigBasket bbdaily delivery man, who drops off two litres of milk each day as part of our subscription. He doesn't ring the bell, but simply leaves the pouches in the bag we hang outside the door.

Ma uses half a litre to make paneer, half for setting curd and the rest for tea, coffee or to pour over cornflakes.

'It is the police,' Ma says.

'Police? During lockdown?' I ask.

'Well, I guess I need to open the door,' she mumbles.

She opens it and I hear heavy footsteps.

'Madam, is anyone at home?' a voice asks.

'I am,' Ma replies equably.

'I mean any *male* member?'

'Why—do women not count in your estimation?' she asks sharply.

She is in her element now. The poor man does not know she is the Head of the Department of Women's Studies at the University of Delhi. She is not going to be quashed by a mere police officer.

'Sir, I am here,' I say loudly.

'Come here, please,' he rasps, all social niceties forgotten.

I pick up my crutches and hobble into the drawing room before Ma can explain I am not exactly mobile. She glares at me balefully—she's been enjoying her altercation with the policeman and she does not want it to end.

He looks at me questioningly.

'Has there been a complaint?' I ask.

He sizes me up for a long time, then asks, 'About what?'

'The drone.' I am glad to get it off my chest. I cannot think why else he is here.

'The drone?' He raises his eyebrows, which are bushy, I notice. 'Do you know you cannot fly a drone without a licence?'

'I know. My brother has one,' I say.

'Let me speak to your brother,' he says.

I murmur, 'He is not here. He left for Delhi a fortnight ago and got stranded because of the lockdown.'

'Thank goodness he has only left Mumbai, and not this world.' He guffaws at his own quip.

I did not know policemen had a sense of humour. I

give a weak smile while my mother glares at him. This kind of remark is not funny, not in the time of the COVID-19 pandemic.

The inspector rings up Abhishek Bhaiya.

'Inspector Shekhawat here,' he says, and speaks to him at length.

Bhaiya blows his fuse on hearing that I have been flying the drone. He calls for me, raves and rants, and promises to flog me—forgetting that he is on speakerphone.

I remind him. He calms down immediately.

'Boys will be boys,' says the inspector indulgently.

He clearly does not think I am a criminal—not with a fractured leg. But I still do not know the purpose of his visit.

'Your neighbour has been murdered,' he says. He sounds almost gleeful delivering the news.

'Mr Tripathi?' Ma asks immediately.

'The one with the telescope?' I say at the same time.

'You must be a Peeping Tom. Otherwise how would you know about the telescope?' he says with a chuckle.

The inspector talks a lot. Perhaps he likes the sound of his own voice.

'How do you know about the telescope?' he asks again.

'It was because of the drone.' I blush. 'I was bored. I dragged myself to the balcony and started flying it. I saw him with his telescope.'

Inspector Shekhawat sprawls in the armchair and asks Ma about our neighbours.

Ma purses her lips and says, 'Mr Das and the Chaubeys live above us. Dr Dwivedi and the Mehtas live below. And Mr Tripathi lives on the side.'

'You know a lot about your neighbours,' he comments.

Ma blushes. 'I called them over for tea to celebrate Yatharth's birthday.'

'I am not a child. I am seventeen,' I growl.

He smiles. He suspects Ma is a curious soul and that a birthday was just an excuse to size up the neighbours.

'So, what can you tell us about them?' he asks.

She frowns as she thinks. 'I like Mr Das. He is young and rather nice-looking.'

I begin to giggle. 'He has a bald spot on top of his head,' I say.

'I have never seen it,' Ma says indignantly.

'That's because he is very tall,' I respond.

Ma ignores me. 'He is friendly. He always says hello if he sees me in the lift or the lobby.' Then she adds, 'He works in a bank.'

'Which bank?' asks the inspector.

'I do not remember. Maybe Bank of India, Indian Bank or perhaps Central Bank. They all sound alike,' she says dismissively.

'He has a dragon tattoo on his neck. Maybe he was inspired by *The Girl with the Dragon Tattoo*,' I add.

'The Chaubeys work in some FMCG—maybe Coca-Cola or HUL or GlaxoSmithKline. I cannot remember,' says Ma.

'They all sound the same,' says the inspector.

She looks at him suspiciously. She suspects he is mocking her. But his face is bland.

'They are snobbish,' she says somewhat peevishly.

I intervene. 'That's not true. They just keep to themselves.'

I know she is miffed because they left soon after arriving at the birthday party, and she didn't get a chance to chat properly.

'Then there was Mr Tripathi.'

'The one who got murdered,' I add.

'He was a reticent man who kept to himself. He never smiled, although he was my next-door neighbour,' says Ma.

'Didn't say hello,' mutters Inspector Shekhawat.

'Exactly,' says Ma. 'He moved here recently,' she adds.

'While we don't live here at all—we are just stranded,' I interject.

Ma ignores me again. 'Dr Dwivedi, who lives below, is a doctor,' she says. She knows because she ran to him when I fractured my leg. He had explained that he was not an orthopaedic, but Ma belongs to the old school—she believes a doctor is a doctor and should know everything.

'He has two large warts on his face,' I add. I have got nothing else to say about him.

'Mr Mehta is a lawyer. He specializes in property law,' says Ma.

'You are a mine of information,' says the inspector.

Ma beams. 'Unfortunately, a week after his birthday, Yatharth fractured his leg. Then the lockdown was imposed.''Two murders in three weeks—not bad,' I say.

Inspector Shekhawat smiles at my ghoulish delight.

Ma shudders. 'What a neighbourhood,' she mutters.

'When did this happen?' Her eyes glint as she asks.

'Yesterday,' he says. 'When the man from BigBasket came to deliver milk this morning, he saw yesterday's milk packets still lying in the bag outside. He rang the bell three times. When there was no response, he informed the lobby. After all, where could Mr Tripathi have gone during the lockdown? They must have tried him on the intercom repeatedly, and when there was still no response, they opened the door and found him dead.'

'We also use the milk subscription service. The delivery men never ring the bell; they simply drop the packets into the bag we hang outside for that purpose. We are not disturbed.'

'That must be how he did it,' says the inspector. 'If the BigBasket man delivered the milk in the morning, and the murderer came later, rang the bell and said "BigBasket", Tripathi would have opened the door without suspicion.'

'And the murderer would have been waiting to kill him,' I say with gory delight.

Inspector Shekhawat turns his attention to me. I have the drone, and he thinks maybe it caught something. I show him the photos. The drone could barely capture anything—just balconies. In some houses, it managed to snap a sofa or a showcase through a half-drawn curtain.

'That's disappointing,' he says.

'Not my fault,' I say petulantly, tugging at my lower lip.

'Well, did you find the murder weapon?' I ask.

Ma interjects. 'Maggi noodles for lunch?'

We have plenty of Maggi at home. I wave her away. I have better things to talk about. Like murder.

'I need to borrow your drone,' says the inspector.

I splutter, 'But what will I do without it?'

'Surely for one day, you can study instead,' he wheedles.

Mother raises her eyebrows. Me? Study during lockdown? Impossible. I never study.

The inspector takes his leave. But Ma is not ready to let him go so easily.

She lambasts him. 'Our next-door neighbour has been murdered. What if someone enters our house and murders me?'

'Well, you have a strapping young lad in the house to protect you,' he quips.

'He has a fractured leg—how can he protect me? You should post a constable outside my house,' she says immediately.

'You do not really expect strangers to come up to your house during lockdown?' he replies.

'Ha! Then how did Mr Tripathi get murdered?' she counters.

He flushes.

'Until you catch the murderer, I shall have sleepless nights,' she adds.

The inspector posts a constable outside Mr Tripathi's house, and Ma has to be satisfied with that.

He is back the next day. Mr Tripathi's house has been dusted for fingerprints and is being thoroughly searched for clues. He drops into our house. He probably treats me like his protégé. Lockdown is a time of little crime. I probably provide him with entertainment.

He brings a lot of photographs with him. They have been retrieved from the drone's memory card. I look at them carefully. I cannot see a possible murder weapon.

'Maybe he carried the murder weapon with him,' I suggest.

I sort through the photos and stack them together. I am obsessed with orderliness. 'See this brass statue?' I say excitedly.

It is a heavy brass statue of Lord Shiva. 'It was there for three days, but it is missing in the latest photograph.'

'Where could it have gone?' wonders Inspector Shekhawat.

The next day I ring him up excitedly. He comes over. I look at him triumphantly.

'Voilà! The statue that was missing from Mr Tripathi's house is now in someone else's showcase!' I declare.

He looks at me doubtfully. 'These statues must be a dime a dozen. Maybe they both bought it from the mall—or even from an exhibition held in your apartment complex.'

'You can always test it for blood. I think you can still find traces, even if it has been washed,' I say.

He smiles at me. 'Seeing detective shows has its advantages,' he murmurs.

He has guessed, quite correctly, that I am an avid fan of crime serials.

He quizzes me about how I use the drone and makes me demonstrate it. He now has a fair idea of the houses the drone covers.

Ma enters the drawing room just then with cups of tea and Marie Gold biscuits. We have chocolate Bourbon biscuits as well, but I suppose in Ma's estimation, the inspector does not deserve them.

The six houses Inspector Shekhawat has narrowed down to are the Chaubeys', Mr Das's, ours, Mr Tripathi's, Dr Dwivedi's and the Mehtas'.

'Who could it be?' I muse, while Inspector Shekhawat breaks off a piece of biscuit and dips it into his tea.

'Mr Chaubey,' says Ma promptly.

'And why is that?' he asks curiously.

'Well,' she says, pursing her lips, 'perhaps it is a love affair gone wrong. Maybe he was unhappy with his wife. I believe the girl who drowned in the pool was very pretty.'

'Why not Dr Dwivedi or Mr Mehta?' I growl.

'He is a doctor,' she says sanctimoniously. 'They save lives.'

'Bah!' I retort. Inspector Shekhawat's eyes twinkle. 'And the lawyer?' he asks blandly.

'Would a lawyer, who is quite conversant with the law, leave a murder weapon in plain sight?' she replies. 'If indeed the Shiva statue is the murder weapon,' she adds.

'My money is on Mr Das,' I say.

'And why is that?' asks the inspector.

I have no answer.

Inspector Shekhawat visits the four houses on the pretext of asking a few more questions. He finds the statue of Shiva in only one house, picks it up for analysis and drags Mr Das to the police station for questioning.

'That nice Mr Das—I am sure you are wrong,' says Ma when she learns of this. 'He is a helpful and friendly man,' she insists. 'He is usually out for an early-morning walk or a late-night swim. I see him by the pool or while returning from my walk.'

Her words are very revealing. Everything falls into place.

Mr Tripathi must have been on the balcony with his telescope, gazing at the stars at night, when he looked down at the pool. He must have seen a girl and a man—with a dragon tattoo on his neck, or perhaps a bald spot on top of his head. But he would not have realized the significance of what he saw. Soon after that, the lockdown was announced.

When he saw the same man later—perhaps in the lobby—with the same tattoo and the same bald spot, there must have been a flash of recognition in his eyes. He must have said, 'Didn't I see you that night, with the lady who drowned in the swimming pool that very night?'

Those words must have sealed his fate.

Mr Das, realizing that Mr Tripathi had recognized him, must have decided to act quickly. So the next morning, after the delivery boy had left the milk at the doorstep, he must have rung the doorbell and called out, 'BigBasket.'

And when the door was opened, he must have entered the house and, seeing the statue, clubbed Mr Tripathi with it.

'That is a lot of conjecture,' says Ma. She refuses to accept that Mr Das could be anything but nice.

'Why would he murder the girl?' she asks plaintively.

'It must be a love affair gone wrong,' says the inspector.

I realize he must be a romantic at heart. 'Maybe he had something to hide,' I say darkly.

I like murders, mysteries, mayhem, subterfuge and espionage—although I admit regretfully that such scenarios are rare.

A day later Inspector Shekhawat returns. He has arrested Mr Das.

'Why did he commit the murder?' I ask excitedly.

The inspector tells me I was right. He had something to hide. He was guilty of bank fraud, and the lady he murdered worked in the same bank. She had discovered it and was about to blow the whistle.

Ma looks downcast while I feel triumphant.

No—to be honest—I preen.

24

Why Did I Forget?

I feel bone-weary all the time. At times I just want to curl up like a foetus in its mother's womb. Sometimes I wish to shut my eyes and hope I do not have to open them again. I want to leave everything behind—the tiny one-bedroom hovel I call home, where the water trickles every morning in driblets, taking forever to fill just one bucket; where rats scurry up and down the floorboards and scamper about the house; where the electricity is as erratic as the water supply.

My life does have its compensations. Whenever I return from work, I look up at our tiny balcony and see Charu waving to me. Her face glows with anticipation. She eagerly awaits my return, even though she knows I will come home empty-handed, not even a toffee in my bag. I am saving up for a scooter. If I had one, Charu and I could travel through the countryside. We could walk amidst green fields, go to Gopalpur-at-Sea, race down the beach and splash about in the waves. Or we could simply squat on the sand and savour coconut water straight from the shell or eat jhalmuri—spicy puffed rice with onions, green chillies, groundnuts and mustard oil. Just mother and daughter by ourselves.

We could even go to Puri one day. I had once thought of buying a second-hand car but Charu talked me out of it. She has taught me how to downsize my dreams.

The thought makes me smile.

I wonder how long it will take me to buy the scooter. It is difficult on a nurse's salary, but nothing can stop me from dreaming. When Charu and I make plans, she smiles. Her face, usually grave beyond her years, lights up and she looks like a little child. Charu is twelve years old. Where did her childhood vanish?

I have no idea.

It got lost in the largely forgettable days that make up our lives.

I am not to blame for the way life turned out. Mohan is. I think of him and frown. It is so easy to blame someone else for one's problems, especially if he is not around.

Mohan is no more. He has no one to blame but himself for his death. People call him brave. I call him foolhardy. And irresponsible. It is all right to play the hero in movies. Why do it in real life?

His death was in vain. One of his friends got into difficulty while swimming at Gopalpur, and Mohan had jumped in to rescue him. He got caught in a whirlpool. Gopalpur is known for whirlpools. I do not know the details. I only know that his body was discovered along with Saransh's.

I was dry-eyed at Mohan's funeral. I did not grieve his death. All I could think of was the mountain of debt he had left behind and the challenge of bringing up a six-year-old daughter alone. The tears came later, and once they did, they never stopped. I cursed him—for leaving me a widow at thirty-two, for burdening me with the loan for the house he had purchased and for condemning me to a lifetime of loneliness.

I needed him. I wanted him beside me. I did not want to consign his remains to the Ganges.

Thank God I had Ma. She left her village to look after Charu while I figured out how to earn a living. It was a toss-up between teaching and nursing, but I chose nursing. I was a science graduate, and the thought of handling a classroom full of brats appalled me. Besides, a nurse works just three days a week—though the shifts are punishing.

The nursing degree took me away from home, but Ma was there to look after Charu. After I qualified, I found a job in a hospital near home. I could cycle or even walk. I liked my work. I thought I was saving lives, or at least helping to do so. Maybe I had always wanted to be a doctor. Ma passed away last year. She was just sixty-six. I thought it was too young to die.

'Papa was just thirty-nine,' Charu said.

'He chose to die,' I replied.

'I wonder what you would have done in his place,' Charu said quietly.

For once, I had no answer.

Luckily, by the time Ma died, Charu was old enough to be a latchkey child. *When did she grow up to be so responsible?*

I had no idea what she did the whole day. I had little time for her when I was working—my shifts were long and Charu was at home by herself. I wondered how she spent the time in my absence.

Today I had a twelve-hour shift, from 7 a.m. onwards. I was tired and my feet were aching. When I left, Charu was still sleeping. I looked at her with affection but didn't have the heart to wake her. It was Saturday—a school holiday. But all day, I had a nagging feeling I was forgetting something. I frowned, trying to remember. I should've kept a note of my tasks. I racked my brains, but nothing came to mind.

When my shift was nearly over and I was looking forward to going home, a boy was brought in with what looked like minor injuries. But his mother was a politician—contesting the Assembly elections. Her face stared down at me from posters across the city. I groaned. A VIP case. Now I would not be allowed to leave.

The boy had injured himself while playing cricket. He had a sprained leg and some bruises—nothing his mother could not have taken care of at home. But she wanted her son to be looked after in a hospital. Attending to him was tiring. His mother was always around, barking orders. Being docile is difficult when one is at the end of one's tether. But I needed this job.

I rubbed a tired hand across my face. What would I not give for a warm bed and a few hours of sleep! I needed to be home, but I knew I would not be able to leave.

I glanced at my watch impatiently. The nurse for the next shift should have arrived by now; the head matron informed me she was delayed. I would have to carry on.

I hoped Charu would eat and go to bed. Thank God Charu was self-sufficient. She made her own meals when I did not have the time and she also got ready for school by herself.

I sighed. By the time she woke tomorrow, I would be home. She would not miss me. In the morning, I would ask her to make a cup of coffee for me—that would take away all the tiredness.

After checking on my patient, I went to the nursing station.

Just then the matron called out, 'One more patient.'

Her voice, usually strident, was unexpectedly kind.

I turned—and the colour drained from my face.

My neighbour Kavya was seated on a bench, and beside her was a girl in a familiar blue frock—one I'd mended only the day before.

'Charu! What happened?' I shouted, running to her.

'She fell from the balcony,' Kavya said sombrely.

'The balcony? How could you—?' I asked, stunned.

'I was leaning on the railing,' Charu said in a small voice. 'I didn't know I'd fall... I didn't think I'd break my hand.'

'Oh my God—how will you manage?'

'Fractures heal in six weeks,' she muttered, sullen.

'Why were you leaning over in the first place?'

Charu said, 'You were supposed to come home... but you didn't. I waited till 7.30 p.m. I was looking out when I lost balance.'

Had she been just leaning—or did she jump? The thought shook me.

'You should have just gone to sleep instead of waiting for me,' I reprimanded her.

'I wanted to spend time with you today,' she murmured.

'What is so special about today?' I asked.

Her voice turned sad. 'You do not remember, do you? It is my birthday.'

And just like that—I knew.

That was what had been niggling at me all day. My daughter's birthday.

What kind of mother forgets her own child's birthday?

'A mother whose daughter chose to injure herself just to see her,' said a quiet voice inside my head.

Suddenly, I couldn't see her clearly any more.

The tears that flowed had blurred everything.